Sherlock Holmes
and the
Pandemic of Death

[Being another manuscript found
in the dispatch box of Dr. John H. Watson
in the vault of Cox and Co., Charing Cross,
London]

Book Seven in the Series,
"Sherlock Holmes and the American Literati"

As Edited By

Daniel D. Victor, Ph.D.

Paperback ISBN 978-1-78705-793-7
ePub ISBN 978-1-78705-794-4
PDF ISBN 978-1-78705-795-1

Published by MX Publishing
335 Princess Park Manor, Royal Drive,
London, N11 3GX
www.mxpublishing.co.uk

Cover design Brian Belanger

Also by Daniel D. Victor

The Seventh Bullet:
The Further Adventures of Sherlock Holmes

A Study in Synchronicity

Sherlock Holmes and the Shadows of
St Petersburg

The Literary Adventures of Sherlock Holmes,
Volumes 1 and 2

Other Books in the Series,
Sherlock Holmes and the American Literati:

The Final Page of Baker Street

Sherlock Holmes and the
Baron of Brede Place

Seventeen Minutes to Baker Street

The Outrage at the Diogenes Club

Sherlock Holmes and the London Particular

The Astounding Murder at Cloverwood House

Dedicated to all who suffered during
the COVID-19 Pandemic, to the health-care workers who
treated them, to the front-line workers who made daily
living possible, and to the scientists who helped
develop a vaccine to end it.

Acknowledgements

Many thanks to Mark Holzband who inspired my thinking; without his idea this story would never have materialized. Thanks also to Seth Victor, whose research led him, his brother, and me to Sauk Centre, Minnesota, and the home of Sinclair Lewis. Thanks to Ethan Victor, whose insightful suggestions about writing are helpful across all genres. Thanks to Richard Evidon for his always perceptive opinions on music, to Barry Smolin and to Sandy Cohen for their valuable editorial advice, to Gabriella Rader for her encouragement, and to Judith Grabiner for her continued help and motivation. And, as always, thanks to Norma Silverman for her patience, support, and love.

[The] very exercise of reflecting on an epidemic from within it is one of the coping mechanisms to which humans have repeatedly turned to make sense of our experiences during these difficult moments.

--Hannah Marcus
"Revisiting the Plague
in the Age of Galileo"
Isis
December 2020

A note on the text:
All headnotes, footnotes, and chapter titles were
added to Dr. Watson's manuscript by the editor,
as was the title of the work itself.

Chapter One

The American Caller

Few and far between were the occasions when my friend and colleague, Mr. Sherlock Holmes, expressed concern about my well-being. I savour them all.

Astute readers will remember that after I had been shot by the American gangster Killer Evans, Holmes rushed to my side, genuinely fearing I had been wounded more severely than I had. When Holmes had experimented with a noxious poison called the Devil's-foot root and almost killed us both in Cornwall, he admitted most gratifyingly that his behaviour was unbecoming a friend. Nor shall I forget his deeply-appreciated confession to feeling "lost" without his Boswell. I treasure all these expressions of closeness, yet only in the case related to the frightening influenza of 1918 can I recall that

9

Holmes actually backed away from an investigation in order to gainsay my guilt.

Allow me to state from the beginning that even the most trifling of references to the ghastly Spanish flu—or the Spanish Lady, as some more crudely call it—arouse in me the deepest feelings of remorse. As a consequence, it is little wonder that readers will search my narratives in vain for any specific references to that terrible disease.

Nor am I alone in such thinking. Although the worst of the pandemic coincided with the end of the Great War, readers are similarly hard-pressed to find mention of the flu's deadly toll in the plethora of histories and memoirs that recount the end of the hostilities.

I for one have found little mystery in the disinclination among such writers to revisit the terror. To me, it has always seemed obvious that those who physically survived the pandemic of '18 purposely erased from their collective memory the dread associated with having confronted so lethal a disease. It was as if the act of forgetting began as soon as the dying had ended.

Unfortunately, my own case was even more dismal. For me, the horror did not stop with the ebbing of the flu; I had an additional abhorrence to face. For entwined with the tragic stories raised by the disease was the relentless guilt I suffered for having believed that through sheer stupidity I had caused the senseless death of a friend.

How annoying then to acknowledge the arrival at my door of a determined American writer whose search for details about a fatal disease inadvertently resurrected the memories I had worked so hard to repress, memories deleterious enough to eclipse not only the mistakes for which I held myself accountable, but also for the greater horrors suffered by countless others.

Neither the falsely-presumed demise of Holmes at the Reichenbach Falls nor even the death of my beloved wife Mary had caused me to spiral downward as did the reckless belief in my own malfeasance during the pandemic, a malfeasance which the American visitor so persistently forced me to confront.

In May of 1926, the American writer, Sinclair Lewis, refused his country's Pulitzer Prize for Best Novel. Arguing that the lure of such awards might entice other authors to alter or modify their works for the primary purpose of winning just such a prize, Lewis rejected the honour. As he explained in his letter to the Pulitzer committee, the desire to win an award like the one he was rejecting encourages

American writers to remain "safe, polite, obedient, and sterile."

To be sure, some critics suggest that Lewis's true motivation was his anger at the Pulitzer committee for not having honoured his novel *Main Street* years earlier. Yet one must also acknowledge that many of his contemporaries continue to regard Lewis's rebelliousness as an act of literary courage.

I certainly do. In fact, though not precisely a demonstration of defiance on my part, I have no doubt that it was Lewis's show of strength that provided me the will to make public the lingering shame I had steadfastly associated with the Spanish flu. In fact, it was but a month after the American's bold rejection of the Pulitzer that I set about to compose this very narrative.

Lewis's personal involvement in my evolution actually began on a crisp afternoon in early March of '23, three years prior to his controversy with the Pulitzer committee. The insistent clanging of the electric bell at my Queen Anne Street door that day caused my young housekeeper, Miss Ross, to hurry in response.

Despite the decline in my hearing, I happened to be leaning on my stick by the entry hall as she opened the door and was thus in an advantageous position to hear an American accent proclaim, "I want to see Dr. John Watson."

"Who should—?" Miss Ross attempted to ask, but the poor woman could not complete the question.

"I am Sinclair Lewis," the man at the door interrupted, enunciating each word as if the appellation were an Open Sesame.

Although his identity meant nothing to Miss Ross, I immediately recognized the name. After all, at that very moment, two of the man's satirical novels, *Main Street* and *Babbitt*, were earning international fame for the prickly American.

"Allow me," I told the housekeeper.

The dependable Miss Ross had been working at Queen Anne Street long enough to tolerate the strange characters—most commonly, personages associated with earlier Holmes cases—who might come round. As a result, in such situations she would ask them in; inform me of their presence; and, as in this instance, immediately disappear.

I was about to invite the visitor to enter when, no sooner had Miss Ross vanished, than the tall and gangling fellow presumptuously stepped inside on his own. Wrapped as he was in a long, black cape, he cut quite the memorable figure. What is more, when he raised a hand in salutation and the cape fell open, I could clearly see its bright purple lining as well as the smartly-tailored black suit, blue bowtie, and white spats that completed his rakish attire.

Equally riveting was the man's pink and pock-marked face. On its right side there appeared a burn-like scar—the result, I should imagine, of a medical attempt to resolve an extreme case of acne. He appeared to be close to forty; and with his ice-blue, gimlet eyes and tufts of ginger hair asserting themselves from under a flat cap of black-and-white tweed, he presented quite the striking image.

"Good afternoon, Mr. Lewis," I said, angling sideways whilst still foolishly trying to usher him in.

"Thanks, John," he addressed me with shocking American familiarity. Removing his cap to reveal his carrot-coloured hair, he added, "They call me Red."

My lanky visitor followed me into the study—actually, my ground-floor library in which I had repositioned my upstairs desk. The move was a way to minimize the need for stair-climbing in light of my gamy knee. I took my place in the turning-chair behind the desk and offered Lewis one of the two wingchairs opposite. Tossing his cape and cap onto the empty seat beside him, he folded himself by sections into the chair I had indicated.

"It's just gone four," I said. "Might I offer you some tea? I'll summon the girl."

"Rather have whisky," Lewis responded. "With soda." As if requiring an excuse, he reminded me, "Such stuff's illegal in the States, you know."

A bottle of Arthur Bell's finest stood nearby; and employing the gasogene to add the fizz, I joined Lewis in the refreshments.

"How I can be of service?" I asked after we both had sampled our drinks. Though I had retired years earlier and now no longer hung a plaque upon my door, I rather naively assumed he had come for medical reasons.

Sinclair Lewis returned to his whisky, his long fingers circling the glass. "Actually, John, if you're open to it, I've come to bat around a few ideas with you concerning my latest novel."

Although his continued familiarity still grated, I confess that I was flattered. The idea that so celebrated an author, especially one noted for his barbs against what he considered the pompous British literati—"smugly content," he had described them— could be interested in my opinion of his work never crossed my mind. Even so, I felt compelled to remind him that I was not a writer of fiction.

"Oh," he chuckled, "I know what you do. I've been following the adventures of Sherlock Holmes for quite a while now. I reckon it must be more than twenty years since I first read *The Hound of the Baskervilles*." Before I could fully consume the compliment, he surprised me by fitting a monocle to his eye. "I'll have you know," he said, peering at me through his now-magnified blue orb, "the main character in my novel *The Trail of the Hawk* reads one of your stories while duck-hunting. I compared the tracking of the mallards to your descriptions of Holmes trailing after thieves."

"Thank you," I said, feeling my face flush.

"Fine and good," Lewis replied with a wave of his eye-glass. "But *Hawk*'s in the past. It's my latest project I want to focus on now, the novel I've only just begun. By way of background, here's what you need to know."

Whilst Lewis slouched in his chair, I took a drink in preparation. The man seemed to have no limits when it came to talking.

"Ever since I was kid back in Sauk Centre, Minnesota, in the U.S. of A.," he explained, "the medical profession has intrigued me. My father is a doctor. So were my grandfather and one of my uncles. My brother Claude is a surgeon. Why, when I was a student back at Yale, I even thought of going into the profession myself. With such a history behind me, I think you can see why I've often considered writing about doctors."

As one who actually succumbed to the calling, I understood completely.

"Oh, I experimented a bit with Dr. Kennicott in *Main Street*," Lewis said, "but ever since that god-awful flu destroyed so much of the world back in '18, I've been giving more serious thought to a novel that actually champions the medical man. I want to depict a doctor as the hero in a battle against some formidable disease."

Lewis's mention of the deadly pandemic immediately evoked the memory that still traumatized me, and I feared he might somehow stumble upon that very topic.

"As noble as such a project might be, Mr. Lewis," I said defensively, "I confess to you that the Spanish flu is not a subject I particularly want to recall. Not only did I contract the disease myself, but you should know that I lost a dear colleague to its clutches. His death haunts me still."

Lewis offered another dismissive wave of the monocle. "Just hear me out. That's all I ask." He did not wait for my response. "Last summer," he continued, "I went to Chicago to meet up with Gene Debs."

"Eugene Debs, the Socialist?" I asked. "The fellow who continually tries to become your President?"

"That's the fellow," Lewis grinned. "Good to know you've heard of him over here. You see, originally, I was planning to feature him in a novel about the labour movement. Who knows? I still might. With a wink, he added, "It's another reason people call me 'Red'."

I forced a dry chuckle.

"But then I got derailed. What happened was, while I was in Chicago, a medical-friend introduced me to a bacteriologist, a fellow named Paul de Kruif who used to be a professor at the U. of Michigan. Perhaps you've heard of him as well."

"As a matter of fact, I have. I've read about him." I may have been retired, but I still perused the odd medico periodical—*The Journal of American Medicine* chief among them. "De Kruif is one of those microbe hunters at the Rockefeller Institute in New York."

Lewis clapped his hands together, almost spilling his drink. "The very same—though Paul no longer works there. Fired last year for writing an article that attacked their mercenary approach to medicine. Too aware of the marketplace, Paul said. Dollar-chasers. Called their capitalist approach medical 'ga-ga-ism'.

"'Bunk' is what I call it—all those medical mafooskies trying to make their quick bucks. Paul said their materialism cried out to be exposed, and that's what he did. I tell you, his passion is so infectious that he fired me up. We started off talking about my one-time interest in becoming a doctor, and then we moved on to discussing the Spanish flu. Soon we were philosophizing about larger issues like the relationship between science and medicine. 'I ought to write a novel about all this,' I declared. That was back in September."

Lewis paused for a moment, stared into his glass, and changed directions.

"At the same time," he said, "I couldn't stop thinking about that terrible flu. It arrived like an invading army. On account of it, my wife Gracie and I moved back to Minneapolis. We were concerned about our son Wells—named after your H.G., by the way, the greatest living novelist in the world today. In any case, our Wells was just over a year old back in '18, and his mother was worried to death he might catch the thing. We figured the Midwest would be safer than New York."

"I've met H.G. Wells," I had to interject.

Lewis's eyes opened wider. "I hope to meet him myself—maybe on this trip."

Happy to divert the conversation, I rambled on. "H.G.—Bertie—actually helped Holmes and me on a couple of cases—one involving your countryman Stephen Crane and the other dealing with someone who had actually lived in the so-called country of the blind, which Bertie himself made famous in a short story."[*]

Lewis did not seem to hear. "Then again," he reflected, "maybe it wasn't the flu that got me riled up about doctors. Maybe it was just how de Kruif took on those fellows at Rockefeller—I'm calling it the McGurk Institute in the novel, by the way. In either case, I told de Kruif I was writing a morality tale about a medical man, a research scientist

---

[*] See Watson's narratives, *The Baron of Brede Place* and "An Adventure in Darkness."

who's driven to fight disease. His goal is noble, but on his journey to reach it, he discovers how much he has to learn—so much, in fact, that based on how little he knows at the start, I'm thinking of calling the novel *The Barbarian*."

A strange title for a book about a doctor, I frowned, *especially a book that is supposed to champion the modern medical man.*

"John," Lewis laughed, "if you could see the expression on your face. But think about it—the title makes sense. The doctor is going to start out as a kid in some hick country village—the way I did in Sauk Centre. In fact, he's going to fall down so often that I also thought of calling the book *The Stumbler*. You probably don't like that one either."

"It's just that—"

"Hold your horses," the American interrupted. "I'll be the first to admit that it's tough to name a book that hasn't been written yet. But thanks to Paul, I've created some outlines, selected one or two character names, and even composed a few pages. I did try coming up with more generalized titles—*The Destroyer* is one or maybe *The Merry Death*. But even with all those choices, I've got to say that I've always been partial to eponymous titles, the ones that use the names of people in the stories. Dickens had it right, you know—*Nicholas Nickleby, David Copperfield, Oliver Twist.*

"*Main Street* turned out well for you," I reminded him.

"Ah, yes," he said, pointing a finger at me as if to verify my literary acuity. "But I'll never get another title that good, one that's become part of everyday speech."

"Indeed," I said.

"But you know, John, however the title ends up, Paul liked the overall idea so much that he agreed to join me. So now we're working on the novel together. We make an excellent duo. You see, I don't really understand all the experiments and the research that go into fighting disease, and he does. I told him to dramatize 'real science', not the phony stuff you see in the movies."

"It makes perfect sense," I said.

"With Paul's expertise, getting the science right has been the easy part. Why, he's already furnished me with a pair of models for my primary scientist"—suddenly, Lewis broke into an exaggerated German accent— "*ze fictional Max Gottlieb, ze Cherman Jew who mentors ze main character.*"

I was surprised at hearing the dialect. I do not mind admitting it.

"For Gottlieb," Lewis said, returning to his regular voice, "Paul suggested I combine the traits of two of his associates—a physiologist named Jacques Loeb and Paul's former teacher, bacteriologist Frederick Novy. Don't get me wrong—they're perfect as scholars—Paul got that right—but I'm looking for more. I want the hunter tracking his prey—dare I say, *ein detektif seeking ze murderer.*"

At last—in spite of all the seemingly random history and humour, the word "detective" finally revealed where Lewis was leading this discussion.

"In fact," he said in confirmation of my thoughts, "I was hoping you could introduce me to your friend Sherlock Holmes. He's already a presence in the book. You see, based on your descriptions of him, I'm giving Gottlieb a hawklike nose and making him thin and tall and nervous. It goes without saying that he'll inherit Holmes's detecting skills, his hunger for Truth. And for the boobs who don't get it, my narrator's going to come right out and say that Gottlieb would have made an excellent Sherlock Holmes."[*]

What a strange fellow, I thought, yet "Quite admirable" is what I said aloud. "You seem to be making excellent progress."

---

[*] In his essay "Sinclair Lewis, Max Gottlieb, and Sherlock Holmes" (*Modern Fiction Studies*, Autumn 1985), Robert L. Coard identifies Lewis's specific references to the detective.

"Would it were so, John; would it were so." He replaced the monocle before adding, "But, you see, the plot continues to give me trouble."

Curious, I thought, recalling an alternative view of Lewis's plotting skills. In the case in '02 that I titled *The Outrage at the Diogenes Club,* Holmes and I had met another American writer, the late Jack London. At one point, he had told us that Sinclair Lewis was so good inventing plotlines that Lewis actually sold them to other authors who were desperate for ideas. London himself confessed to buying some fourteen. I told my visitor as much.

"I know, I know," Lewis replied, now twirling the monocle. "I'm supposed to be good at these things, but the opening section of this new novel—it moves too slowly. All I really have so far is just a detailed plan." Here his long fingers withdrew a small notebook from an inner coat pocket. "These are my notes."

Riffling through the pages to illustrate his point, Lewis displayed a collection of small yellow sheets filled with lots of scribblings and a number of unrecognizable but detailed maps. One page in particular was headed in block letters that read "BACTERIOLOGICAL NOTES".

The American paused a moment and closed the notebook. "Funny you should mention Jack though," he mused. "Most fitting. I remember I once suggested that he should create a character like

Sherlock Holmes. He could use him in a magazine series about a World Police force I had thought up."

I cocked an eyebrow. Holmes had enough disagreements with Scotland Yard; a world-wide police organization would drive my poor friend mad.

"Jack and I weren't getting along near the end," Lewis remembered. "He claimed I'd published something about him I wasn't supposed to. Pure bunk!"

The man does like to talk, I marvelled once more.

"It's this Spanish flu business," Lewis carried on. "It's too amorphous. From the start I haven't been able to hang a complete storyline around it. That's why de Kruif and I decided to write about the plague. At least, there's a cure for that."

"Thank God," I said.

"Or thank the scientists who found the bacteria responsible. More to the point, de Kruif and I thought that to gain fresh ideas, we should to travel to places where people had suffered a lot. This past January we set out on an old freighter called the *Guiana*. According to my friend, Henry Mencken, Paul and I were both so drunk he had to *pour* us onto the deck. Personally, I can't remember the details. At any rate, we headed for the West Indies. A hundred thousand people died there from flu, you know."

I did not know. It was a staggering figure.

"We began on St. Thomas in the Virgin Islands. In Barbados, we took a Dutch steamer, the *Crynssen*, to Trinidad and then to the north coast of South America. We moved on to Panama and eventually to Plymouth. Now—a little more than two months after we first set out—here we are in London. We arrived a couple of days ago—March sixth, to be precise."

"Welcome to England," I said.

"You might be interested to know that I've made the trip before. But on this visit, I figured it was about time that I met Arthur Conan Doyle."

"My agent."

"Right. After all, the fellow is also a writer, and he lived through the flu. I figured I could gain some insights. But that was before we left. On the boat I read his piece on how the flu had killed his son."

As I have reported elsewhere, unlike many of my colleagues, Sir Arthur publicly announced his own personal tragedy that resulted from the Spanish flu. In yet another of history's grand ironies, his son Kingsley, an army medico—Sir Arthur called him 'a very perfect man"— had barely survived the bloodiest conflict in British military history.

On 1 July 1916, the first day of the infamous Battle of the Somme, he was struck in the neck by two German bullets. Army doctors patched him up and trotted him out to the front lines again where, just weeks before the Armistice, he was killed not by enemy gunfire but by the influenza.

Whilst other fathers might have collapsed at the news, Sir Arthur reaffirmed his faith in Spiritualism. He assured everyone that he was sustained by his belief in the ability to communicate with those who have passed on. It was almost a year later that he experienced what he called "the supreme moment" of his spiritual life.

During a séance, Sir Arthur reported that he heard a familiar voice in the darkened room call, "Father."

"Dear Boy, is that you?" he asked.

In response, he said he felt the breath of a face close to his own, sensed a kiss upon his brow, then heard the voice murmur, "Forgive me."

Sir Arthur maintained that it was Kingsley he had heard requesting forgiveness for doubting the reality of spiritualism. The father asked his son if he was happy; and after a fearful silence, Sir Arthur heard the words he had sought: "Yes, I am so happy."

"Conan Doyle," I told Lewis, "truly believed it was his son who had spoken to him."

"Bunk," replied the American. "I know all about that other-world blather, that world-beyond-the-shade business. Why, I've heard the best of the Holy Rollers, Billy Sunday himself, spin a tale or two.

Even pitched in my own hosannahs with the other saps just to see how it felt." Suddenly, Lewis tilted his head back, opened his mouth wide, and shouted out a fierce whoop.

So loud was his shriek that Miss Ross came running into the sitting room. "Is everything all right?" she asked looking round.

"Everything's fine," I assured her and sent her off.

"My point is," said Lewis, "I'm too practical to fall for those stories about life on the Other Side. I need a more solid approach. That's why I decided to come see you instead, John. I reckoned that you—being a medical man and a gifted chronicler—you might be able to furnish me with some believable stories. I'm looking for tangible details, details that don't come from some fantasy world, details—dare I say? —that are different from the ones I've picked apart in the states."

I shook my head. "I'm certain that the American and British responses to the flu are fairly standard." Hoping to fend off any further questions, I added, "I don't imagine that I have anything new to offer."

Lewis leaned back, balled his hands into fists, and slowly stretched his arms. "Well," he sighed, drawing out the word, "I did already say that I'm hoping you can connect me with Sherlock Holmes. I'm sure," he smiled broadly, "that he must have some original tales to tell about 'The Spanish Lady'."

Sinclair Lewis's red face and leering grin suggested a more eccentric view of the matter than the more sombre approach to which I was accustomed. In fact, the more he joked, the more plentiful in my mind's eye appeared the memories of the sick and dying.

Yet at the same time, I could not deny the sympathy I was feeling for a fellow-author in search of material. I realized that in his place, I would have appreciated any help I could acquire.

"I suppose I can provide you with a few details," I told Lewis reluctantly. "But I cannot speak for Holmes. I do know that he spent most of the pandemic quarantined in the South Downs, so I can't imagine he has much to offer—though he did come here to be my nursemaid after the infernal disease had struck me."

"Take no offense at my interest in Holmes, John," said Lewis. "Obviously, I want to hear your story as well as his."

"In Holmes's retirement," I offered, feeling on firmer ground talking about my friend's experience than my own, "he tends to keep to himself."

"I'm a pretty persuasive fellow," Lewis said, rubbing his hands together. "Why not arrange a meeting for all three of us?"

There was no doubt that Sinclair Lewis could be persuasive; yet even before I answered, he said, "But since I'm here right now, let's begin with you."

I furrowed my brow. Not only did I not want to remember, but I also understood a satirist's ability to skewer his subjects—this satirist's in particular.

Lewis held up his hand. "Not to worry, John. I respect your privacy. I'll never mention your name." He produced a pencil from another pocket, and re-opening the notebook that was resting on his knee, allowed the pencil tip to hover inches above a blank page. "If you don't mind though, I'd like to take down the important facts."

I had already given my approval. There seemed no cause to go back on my word. Besides, it was not his notetaking that had anything to do with the disturbing memories evoked by his questions. It was the memories themselves.

Chapter Two

The Pandemic of 1918

The face of London was now
indeed strangely altered.
— Daniel Defoe
A Journal of the Plague Year

*T*ouching glasses, Sinclair Lewis and I returned to our whiskies. A sampling of spirits seemed as appropriate an action as any other for contemplating not only my own unforgivable failure, but also—and much more significantly—one of the greatest examples of irony in European history.

Though the world continues to commemorate the 1918 Armistice that ended the Great War—the celebrated "eleventh hour of the eleventh day of the eleventh month"—the dying did not stop when the papers were signed. Oh, the guns may have finally ceased their horrific chatter; that cold and bitter East Wind, which Holmes had predicted, may have finally halted its withering blasts; but an enemy far deadlier than the gale Holmes feared continued to howl. The longed-for sunshine he had also foreseen had not yet broken through.

In the forty-six weeks between June 1918 and May 1919, more than 200,000 of my countrymen fell to the influenza—some experts estimate the global sum at fifty million—far more deaths than those caused by the Great War itself. Still others argue the total is significantly higher.

"For the record," I said, pointing to Lewis's notebook, "the Spanish flu didn't gain its name because it originated in Spain or because the Spanish King contracted the illness."

"I know, I know," Lewis said with a dismissive wave. "Spain was a non-combatant. She didn't have to worry about telling the world how effectively the virus was destroying her armies." He put down his pencil and hoisted his glass once again. "To censorship," he said sarcastically; and after finishing his drink, he asked for more.

"As you probably also know from working with de Kruif," said I whilst refilling his glass, "there are many theories as to where the flu got started. Some believe it sprang up in a British military encampment in Etaples, France."

Lewis held up his free hand, the one without the drink, palm facing me. "Not so fast. I think we Americans deserve the credit."

I smiled self-consciously, and he lifted his glass to acknowledge my appreciation.

"There are medical men who maintain that the flu originated in Kansas," he went on. "They think the pigs at a farm in Haskell County passed the disease to the soldiers at a nearby military camp. Others believe that while soldiers were burning manure, they inadvertently inhaled the smoke that infected them."

"It seems reasonable," was all I could think of saying.

Lewis, however, was not yet done. "In another one of his sanctimonious sermons, Billy Sunday denounced the flu as 'the wages of sin'. And would you believe it? No sooner did he say the words than some people collapsed right there in front of him. But you know what? How the flu started doesn't really matter; what's important is that American doughboys carried it across the sea."

"You may be right," I told him, "but however it got to Europe, our British soldiers did some carrying of their own. When they returned from the front, they transported it back to England."

"In three waves, right?"

Nodding, I held up my fingers as I listed them. "In the summer of '18, in the fall of '18, and then again in the spring of '19. By the time it was all over, a million people in London had been afflicted, myself included."

Lewis scribbled some notes. Then he looked up and said, "Tell me about your own experience, John—from beginning to end."

Since discussing "my own experience", as he phrased it, would raise issues I hoped to avoid, I planned to answer Lewis in the most general of terms. "I was a typical victim," I told him. "Age-wise, I was somewhere in the middle. The very young and the very old are the ones who usually contract influenza. But not this time.

"The Spanish flu behaved little like similar diseases of the past. Indeed, the fact that it infected people in the middle range of ages is what made the disease so difficult to identify at first. And because doctors were slow to recognize the illness as influenza, they prescribed only the most general of remedies: take to bed, ingest aspirin, consume fluids, apply a hot poultice on the chest to prevent congestion."

"Right," Lewis agreed. "We tried those treatments in the States as well."

"Sickness multiplied," I continued, "and people turned to all sorts of additional remedies—from cinnamon, camphor, ammonia, eucalyptus and alcohol to beef supplements like Oxo cubes, cough syrups, and heavy doses of salicin.[*]

"There was no specific national plan to speak of. In different cities, Medical Officers had to deal with the disease on their own. They issued broadsheets to illustrate safe behaviours like washing

---

[*] An aspirin-like glucoside found in willow-bark prescribed for reducing fever and headache.

with soap and avoiding handshakes. 'Ventilate public places,' they argued. 'Shutter the schools. Close the cinemas.'"

"We did the same."

"Here in Leicester Square, theatres advertised that their halls were well ventilated and that their stalls were disinfected between film-showings. More directly, doctors instructed people to sanitize their homes, open wide their windows, stay indoors."

"And wear masks," Lewis added, waggling his forefinger.

"Quite right—much good that it did. Notices went out instructing people to cover their faces, though many, including doctors, ignored the order. It seemed as if everyone had to be constantly reminded that germs travel in the air, that coughing, sneezing, and even speaking spread the flu."

"In New York and Chicago," Lewis said, "you could get fined for sneezing in public."

"To be fair, lots of people did employ cotton handkerchiefs or wide strips of gauze although curiously they often left their noses uncovered. Some resorted to paraphernalia that looked like military gas masks. And one cannot forget the woollen nose plugs."

"In San Francisco," Lewis added, "there were gunfights with people who wouldn't wear masks— 'mask-slackers,' we called them."

"Slackers," I nodded, "a good word. It links people who refused to wear masks with those who refused to perform their military duties."

Lewis did some more writing. "What else?" he said. "Tell me something I haven't thought of."

I pondered his request for a moment. "What about the Turkish baths?" As soon as I uttered the words, I remembered Nevill's in Northumberland Avenue that Holmes and I used to frequent. It was in the wood-panelled drying-room many years before that I had first met Samuel Clemens.*

"Nevill's was a popular destination," I told Lewis. "Even today they promote their ventilated steam rooms as suitable for curing influenza. Of course, if one desired privacy during the pandemic— and could afford it—one might purchase an individual steam bath for the home, wooden sweat boxes that leave only the head exposed."

"An individual steam bath," Lewis murmured. "Give me a moment," he said, and on one of the blank yellow pages of his notebook he silently sketched a simple outline of the box I had just described.

"People bought disinfectants which they gargled," I went on, "and balls of carbolic-acid whose vapours they inhaled. There was opium or heroin to

---

* Watson describes the meeting in the case he titled *Seventeen Minutes to Baker Street.*

ease people's coughs. Children wore small bags of camphor round their necks. I suppose that if nothing else, such remedies served the purpose of making their users feel they were helping themselves recuperate. Here in my own house, I retained the services of Miss Ross. I needed the help. When she went out, she wore a mask; inside, we kept our distance."

"Well done, John," Lewis said, looking up from his notes. "You enabled a member of the working class to keep her job. Gene Debs would be proud. We must never forget workers like your Miss Ross—people who face the greatest dangers in order to preserve our own way of life."

"Sad but true," I agreed. "Shops needed staffing. Trains, trams, and omnibuses needed running. Yet with so many working-people ill, there were fewer places open and a decrease in public transports. The result was greater crowding and a consequent spreading of influenza."

"Just like at home, "Lewis laughed. "Things got so bad that kids invented a jump-rope chant." He flipped back through his yellow pages till he found the words he was seeking. Then he picked up his glass and waved it in time to the singsong cadence:

I had a little bird.
Its name was Enza.
I opened up a window,
And in-flew-Enza.

"Children here in England did the same," I smiled, fully aware that the longer we spoke in historical generalities, the longer I could prevent talking about my own pathetic role in the tragedy. Yet Sinclair Lewis was a perceptive writer who craved specific facts to humanize his story. Perhaps he even discerned that I was holding back. At the very least, he understood it was time to personalize the drama.

"You reported that you yourself suffered through the flu," Lewis said. "How did that come about?"

I sighed resignedly. "From the start, I recognized the role that retired medicos could play. At the beginning of 1918, more than half of our medical people were already serving in the military. By the spring, the conscription age for doctors was over fifty. According to the experts, so many of our doctors and nurses had travelled with the army to the front that some sixty percent of those with fatal cases of flu here at home never had the opportunity to see a doctor.

"As a result, third- and fourth-year medical students were sent into hospital wards. Retired doctors were called back into service. I was no different," I explained to Lewis. "I wanted to help, and so I volunteered."

Chapter Three

The Queen Anne Street Laboratory

Even the company of the mad
was better than the company of the dead.
--Stephen King
The Stand

"*B*y 1918," I told Sinclair Lewis, "I had been retired for three years. Yet in good conscience, no one, especially a doctor, could ignore the devastating impact of the flu. It was the widespread severity of the illness that was so alarming.

Convinced that more help was needed, I set out in August—just days following my sixty-sixth birthday—to confront the deadly disease. Dressed like many another independent colleague in top hat, frock coat, and white cotton mask, I prepared myself for battle against the pandemic of death.

"In the name of familiarity, I decided to begin with the patients I could locate from my former Kensington surgery. It had been close to thirty years since I had seen them, and a significant number had suffered natural deaths in the interval. In 1918, of course, the Spanish flu had killed many others.

"In point of fact, most of the few I did manage to find turned out to be adults I had treated as children. In the end, however, who they were and how much they were suffering proved of little consequence. For by early September, my arthritic knee began barking; and whilst guilt-ridden over giving up my newly-developed responsibilities, I found it too difficult to carry on."

As I spoke, the memory of the pain caused me to rub the patella of my right knee.

"Yet even with my disability," I said to the American, "I would not allow myself to give up the fight; I would simply choose a more stationary assignment. Once more I sought out the familiar by volunteering to work at St. Bartholomew's, the oldest teaching hospital in London and the institution where, as a houseman, I received much of my medical training."

Lewis pointed a finger at me. "And where, if I'm not mistaken, you met your friend Sherlock."

My eyebrows shot up in dismay. This time the American had gone too far. "I must tell you, sir—Sherlock Holmes does not appreciate being referred to by his Christian name."

Lewis waved his monocle as if to move me along. "You were telling me about St. Bart's."

"Yes," I said, drawing a deep breath. "Dr. Timothy Glass was my superior, a haggard figure, as I remember him in 1918, walking about in a white mask and well-worn lab coat, a black patch covering his right eye—there had been some sort of accident years before. The visible eye was sad and solitary; and with his salt-and-peppered hair, he looked every bit the distressed administrator tasked with the impossible assignment of halting the inexorable march of the influenza.

"On the occasion of our first meeting, I found him before the open door of his office. As it happened, he was involved in an intimate discussion with a strikingly handsome, square-jawed gentleman incongruously sporting a red carnation in his lapel. Over six-feet tall and straight-backed in black tailcoat, grey waistcoat, striped trousers, and grey spats, the fellow wore no mask. In fact, he appeared to be preoccupied with the smoke he was inhaling from a cigarette.

"I had recognized him immediately, of course. Though he often tried shielding his face from cameras to protect his privacy, candid photographs frequently found their way into the public prints along with the odd portrait taken by a stylish photographer in the West End. This was the celebrated pathologist, Dr. Bernard Spilsbury."

"I've heard of him," Lewis said. "I believe he was knighted just before de Kruif and I left on our trip to the West Indies.   Is he not *Sir* Bernard now?"

"Just so. It was only last December when he himself learned that his knighthood would be announced in the New Year's Honours. The award was granted at the behest of Prime Minister Bonar Law for services rendered to the Crown. Such is the reward for the thousands of post-mortems Spilsbury has conducted as the primary pathologist to the Home Office, not to mention the countless courtroom analyses he has scrupulously delivered as a witness for the prosecution."

"That good, eh?" Lewis asked.

"To be sure. And he continues excelling in both roles. It is well-known that Spilsbury likes to immerse himself in the facts of a case; as a result, when his name appears on a post-mortem report that implicates a defendant, the result is tantamount to conviction."

Lewis jotted down more details in his notebook.

"When I saw him that day with Dr. Glass, Spilsbury had not yet come over to Bart's. In '18, he was still doing post-mortems at St. Mary's in Paddington. For two decades, in fact, he had been the chief resident pathologist there, and St. Mary's is considered the best teaching hospital in the country. Yet Sir Bernard allowed a disagreement with a colleague to turn into such a major confrontation that

44

he left the place in November of 1920 for the position at Bart's of lecturer on morbid anatomy and histology."

"Connected with the Crippen case, wasn't he?" Lewis asked.

"Indeed, the very case in which I myself first heard of the man. It was Sherlock Holmes who gave me the details. I should tell you, Mr. Lewis, that in spite of all the notoriety, the complete story of the North London Cellar Murder, as it was then called, has yet to be told."

"North London Cellar Murder," Lewis mumbled as he made another note.

"Holmes's involvement has never been reported. In 1910, at the request of Detective Chief Inspector Walter Dew, he came out of retirement to aid Scotland Yard in the investigation of Dr. Hawley Harvey Crippen."

"Inspector Dew," Lewis mused. "Why, wasn't he the copper who arrested Crippen in Quebec? As I recall, Scotland Yard relied on the new Marconi telegraph system to locate the villain at sea."

"Precisely," I said. "But it was at 39 Hilldrop Crescent, Crippen's address in Camden Town, where Holmes presented his own view of the case to the four pathologists already there. Until then, they had been able to glean nothing from the unrecognizable remains of Crippen's wife found buried beneath the brick floor of the basement.

"As it happened, Holmes's insights on the nature of scarring solidified the murder charges against Crippen. Yet the police gave the credit to the pathologist. Spilsbury, they argued, had detected a scar on a minuscule sample of skin belonging to the deceased. It was the first of many such victories for the pathologist; and as his knighthood confirms, he was hailed by the Home Office as well as by Scotland Yard."

Lewis offered a wry smile. "What's the catch, John? Awards are never so simple."

I had to laugh. "That observation certainly applies in Spilsbury's case. To be sure, he received plaudits for his work. People marvelled at his ambidexterity in performing autopsies, at his adherence to detail in reporting post-mortems, at his acknowledged *sangfroid* in providing testimony.

"But here's the rub. All his subsequent achievements turned out to be Pyrrhic victories. For during the course of his career, the more success he gained, the more he could not escape being associated with my friend. Each of Spilsbury's triumphs reinforced a comparison he could not come out from under. Simply put, Sir Bernard Spilsbury became known as 'The Sherlock Holmes of Medical Detection.'"*

---

* As confirmed by Mark Honigsbaum in *Living with Enza: The Forgotten Story of Britain and the Great Flu Pandemic of 1918*, p. 111.

Lewis pointed his pencil at me. "Another one of those ironies you're so fond of citing."

"A digression might be more apt. Be that as it may, when the conversation at Bart's between Glass and Spilsbury began to wane, Glass motioned for me to join them.

"'Dr. Watson, isn't it?' he asked. 'You've been expected.'

"I confirmed my identity and, because one avoided shaking hands during the pandemic, simply nodded. Glass then introduced me to Spilsbury, but of course I had recognized him already.

"Glass informed me that Spilsbury frequently appeared at Bart's; and as I was about to begin work there, I might encounter the noted pathologist any number of times. I greeted Spilsbury with an abbreviated bow, and he responded by exhaling a cloud of cigarette smoke and offering a curt nod. He then pivoted and, retrieving his black silk top hat from a nearby desk, placed the hat upon his head and marched off, a wisp of smoke trailing behind."

"Not too garrulous a fellow," said Lewis.

I could not disagree. "On the other hand, the harried Dr. Glass did his best to welcome me. He said that the medical staff at Bart's appreciated whatever help they could secure, even though—so far, at least—conditions weren't as bad they had been during the Russian flu in '89.

"I remembered the year. I had just begun my practice in Paddington. Among my long list of patients were many victims of the Russian flu. According to Glass, thousands of sick people would be waiting in queues for treatment outside of Bart's in the morning before staff arrived. 'Thank God,' he said, 'we are not yet that overwhelmed.'"

It was possible, I had supposed at the time, that some of the people infected in '89 might have developed an immunity to the current influenza. As the year progressed, however, such suppositions mattered very little.

"'Let me show you round,' Glass said. Motioning towards a nearby corridor, he warned, 'Be certain your mask is secure.'"

Even though I was trying to be open with Lewis, I realized that I did not care to repeat aloud the horrific scenes I have continued to recall ever since that first day when I followed Glass through the hospital. We had climbed a stone staircase and, beneath a low-arched ceiling, proceeded along a whitewashed corridor until we reached the dun-coloured double-doors of a common ward.

As soon as he had opened them, I was struck by the stinging smell of carbolic acid and urine. But the smells were minor when compared with the shocking sight. The ward was dimly lit. And whilst a handful of white-masked doctors and nurses were hastening back and forth, hundreds of stricken patients lay motionless in measured ranks of dark-metal bedstands. Greying sheets had been hung between a few of the beds in a meagre attempt to maintain privacy and protection. But one could never conceal the row upon row of the sick and dying.

And this was but one of many such wards in but one of many such hospitals throughout the country. Glass had said that the medical staff were "not yet overwhelmed," and yet neither then nor thereafter have I witnessed conditions so dire.

To Lewis, I told a simpler truth—that I had seen numerous beds filled by afflicted patients, many of them on the verge of death.

"And just how were you supposed to treat them all?" Lewis asked.

"A good point. In fact, I posed the same question to Glass."

"'It's tremendously frustrating,' he told me with a sigh. 'To be honest, there's not much we have to offer these poor souls.' He then listed a number of the conventional medicines to which people gravitated on their own: potassium permanganate as a nose-and-mouth wash; quinine for fever; morphine for pain; digitalis to slow the heart."

"Hold on a minute, John," Lewis said. He had written "MEDICINES" in block letters at the top of a blank page and was now furiously copying down the examples I had listed. After a moment, he nodded for me to proceed.

"Glass said there were as many remedies as there were doctors. He knew one doctor who recommended inhaling iodine in steam, another who offered injections of garlic oil dissolved in pure ether, and still another who suggested purging with castor oil. Glass even told me of a doctor who had tried bleeding his patients."

"Sounds like the docs didn't know what to do either."

"You're right," I smiled. "Glass said that the Local Government Board actually admitted that they knew of nothing to halt the influenza's progress. That was the moment when he confessed to me in a whisper that the most common medicine administered at Bart's was brandy."

Sinclair Lewis clapped his hands in delight. "The medicinal remedy for all kinds of problems—even today."

"Glass believed it was as effective as anything else they had to offer. In any case, following our visit to the ward, he escorted me to the research laboratories. I did my best to follow him, but favouring my knee made keeping up difficult. After I fell behind a second time, he addressed my lack of mobility.

"'I shall assign someone to work at your side,' he insisted. 'It appears you could use the help.'

"In fact, no sooner did we enter the nearest laboratory than he summoned a young man who, between puffs of a cigarette, had been huddled over a microscope. Glass called him over, and the fellow, after carefully placing the lit cigarette at the front edge of his workspace, came over and introduced himself. That was how I came to meet Martín Aaron-Smith—a microbiologist in his final year of medical school just down from Oxford."

"Martin Aaron-Smith," Lewis repeated and scribbled the name into his notebook.

"Aaron-Smith was tall and thin," I told Lewis, "with a shock of sandy hair that fell over his brow. He was also, I would soon learn, an outstanding microbiologist. Like the attending doctors, he wore a white coat; yet, like Spilsbury, he remained mask-less in order to smoke. From what I could smell, the cigarette was very strong indeed."

"Aaron-Smith." Lewis repeated the name, and then he vigorously underscored it twice in his notebook. "I like the name—it's strong and rich with possibilities."

"True," I lamented, "like the poor soul himself. If only he had survived the pandemic."

The American looked up but did not pursue that line of questioning just then. Instead, he took another drink, then said, "Tell me about this Aaron-Smith."

"Well, he was an Englishman by birth— born in Chipping Norton. His late father was a doctor—"

"Like mine," Lewis reminded me.

"—a doctor for the men who worked in the mills. It's probably from him that his son developed an interest in medicine. I should also point out the uniqueness of his Christian name."

"Martin?" Lewis questioned.

I shook my head. "Although he was born in the Cotswolds, he actually stressed the second syllable—Martín. His mother was French, you see, and he inherited the pronunciation from her. I might add that it was also from her that he inherited his love of those infernal French cigarettes—*Gauloises, Gitanes*—I'm not certain which. I'm sure it was one of those he was smoking when I first met him at Bart's, the kind with the terrifically strong aroma."

"The kind that stink, you mean," Lewis laughed. "Personally, I smoke Home Runs, an American brand. They provoke the same reaction."

"Though Martín was always smoking those foul things, he was a dedicated scientist; and even though he frequently shunned a mask, I liked him immediately—so much so that after we had worked together at Bart's for a fortnight, mask or no mask, I decided to offer him a kip.

"Martín had just come down from Oxford, and it seemed simpler for him to lodge with me here in Queen Anne Street than to continue renting a room in a neighbourhood which he confessed he didn't know at all. To render the offer more attractive,

I told him I was in the process of setting up a makeshift laboratory in the basement."

"So the two of you could work here together?"

"Exactly.   In fact," I said, pointing downward—"just below where you and I are sitting right now."

"Convenient," Lewis said.

"I wish I could claim prescience, but it was pure chance that not long before the pandemic began, I had electricity installed downstairs with the idea of creating a work area for myself. A gas line was already in place as were a small sink and a slightly-cracked tile floor.

"The new lighting arrived at the same time as the influenza, and I thought of creating a laboratory where I might do medical research.   I ordered a refrigerator to be set up, and I purchased some wooden tables, which I positioned along the back wall beneath a set of shelves. Though climbing the stairs continues to bother me, I asked Miss Ross to move my microscope from here in the sitting room down into my new laboratory.

"Once I told Martín that I had converted my basement into a laboratory, I had little trouble convincing the microbiologist to accept my offer. Trusting the hospital to make a new microscope available to the young man, I invited him to bring his own here to Queen Anne Street so he could continue his research in his new digs. Dr. Glass supplied us with a pair of Bunsen burners along with an assortment of flasks and test tubes.

"Martín joined me at the start of October, and I must say that it was a most suitable arrangement. It required but a day or two to establish a routine. We'd dine first and do our research afterwards. We also travelled to Bart's together. Due to my knee, we generally hailed a cab though there were a few occasions when I felt fit enough to walk. On foot, it required less than an hour to reach the hospital.

"I might also add that as long as Miss Ross could open all the windows in the house to let out the acrid smells of carbolic acid and other such chemicals, we faced no resistance from her. On the contrary, she seemed happy to make the young gentleman feel welcome.

"The plan worked perfectly. Martín referred to himself as my '*garçon*', and I can still picture him at work here. He wore rubber gloves, leather boots, and those leather straps that hold back one's shirtsleeves. But despite my talk of conveniences, Mr. Lewis, let it not be forgotten that we were doing important work—seeking an antidote to the plague that was crushing the nation."

"Plague," Lewis repeated. "Not flu?"

I raised my hands to calm him. "I speak metaphorically," I reassured the novelist. "For plague, there is a cure. For the Spanish flu, alas, there is none—at least, none that anyone has found so far. But that didn't stop Martín and me from looking. Bacteriologists in particular were hoping to discover a phage that would destroy the enemy. Scientists had developed a vaccine to fight smallpox; we could only assume there had to be one to combat influenza."

"If only you could identify the cause," Lewis said.

"Precisely. Most medical men believed the cause to be an as-yet undetected strain of bacterium. 'Pfeiffer's Bacillus'—named for the German who discovered it in the early '90's—was a popular candidate. *Haemophilus influenzae* it was called officially. To be sure, it is toxic, but nowhere near as dangerous as some doctors argued. Even Spilsbury defended its lethality.

"Martín, however, did not. In spite of the prevailing medical opinion, Martín refused to believe that a familiar bacillus like Pfeiffer's could be responsible for so deadly a flu. In truth, he wasn't even convinced that the culprit was a bacterium. It was this speculation that the germ might be something with which we weren't familiar that motivated his search for the true origin of the influenza."

"Quite ambitious, this Martin Aaron-Smith."

"It's probably why he was so fond of quoting Pasteur."

"French roots," Lewis muttered.

"In quoting Pasteur, Martín would raise a forefinger for emphasis and then proclaim, 'The microbe causes the illness. Look for the microbe and you'll understand the illness.'

"*D'accord*," Lewis muttered again.

"Curiosity drove Martín. He was constantly searching, and his compulsion was—if you'll pardon the pun—contagious. For the first half of October, he and I spent many a late hour seeking the deadly germ within the samples of sputum and lung tissue we had collected."

"A dogged detective," Lewis observed, "seeking the possible murderer of the Spanish Lady."

"An appropriate description," said I. "As he worked, Martín would mutter, 'There must be something else, there must be something else.' Among his favourite candidates were 'Filter-passers', sub-microscopic organisms that we have yet to identify. 'I am certain," Martín said, "there is some sort of undetected agent, some virus[*] we can't see,

---

[*] The term "virus" as employed in 1918 was quite different from the word we use today. Broadly speaking, a virus was originally considered a general agent that caused infectious disease. Once the influenza virus was discovered in 1933, however, the term became more specific. It was used to designate the sub-microscopic, pathogenic agent responsible for the influenza infection, an agent capable of increasing rapidly within a living cell.

that travels through the air. Such a microbe must be responsible for all this.'

"I remained unconvinced—not that it mattered—for it was then that I myself contracted the illness. That was in the middle of October in '18. Believe me when I tell you, Mr. Lewis, that once stricken, one loses interest in the origins of the infernal disease. One loses interest in most everything. You see, it's one thing to recognize the symptoms in one's patients—the headaches, the body pain, the sore throat, the running nose, the coughs, the suffocation, the fevers that can run up to 105. I assure you that it's quite another to experience them oneself."

"Similar to pneumonia or bronchitis, I'm told."

I shook my head at his naiveté. "Much, much worse, I'm afraid. Personally, I trace my own susceptibility to the case of enteric fever I contracted during my days in India. I believe the illness weakened my constitution all those years ago and made it that much more difficult for me to fend off the flu.

"Fortunately—though I did not know it at the start—my illness turned out to be less severe than I had expected. Whilst I was suffering, I recall being terrified that my symptoms would grow worse. Let me assure you, Mr. Lewis, fear is a major debilitating factor. Fear can actually encourage the progress of the disease itself.

"I believe it was such fear that prompted me to ask for Sherlock Holmes. Oh, Miss Ross secured the food for the house and kept the place ventilated and cleaned well enough. Even Martín helped attend to my basic needs in the hours he was here. Yet he also needed to continue his research downstairs and had little opportunity to concern himself with me.

"As my agony continued, I managed to convince Martín to ring Holmes for help. It was a Saturday night—the nineteenth of October, I would learn later. I knew that in order to minister to me, my old friend would have to leave the safety of his cottage, and yet I could think of no one else to summon. Of course, he rose to the occasion. In retrospect, I think it was his support that contributed the most to curing me."

"Quite the act of loyalty," Lewis observed.

"An act I shall not soon forget. Sick as I had been for more than a week, I shall forever treasure the sight of Holmes materializing in my bedroom the Monday following Martín's call.

"Like a phantom, Holmes emerged out of the murk. At first, with his face a pale blur, I fancied him a delusion. It took me some time to realize that he was still attired in his outer wear—the Inverness cape and the deerstalker with the flaps pulled down over his ears. But it was the thick, white cotton mask covering the lower half of his face that confused me the most. Only later did I understand that it was not the usual thin-gauze variety.

"'Too porous, old fellow,' Holmes explained when I had asked about it."

Lewis nodded. "I get the picture. You tell quite the story, John—which, of course, is exactly why I'd very much like to hear additional views of these events from Holmes himself."

I appreciated Lewis's desire for more facts; he had a book to write. "I do understand that the time Holmes spent with me could contribute to your research," I told him. "After all, Holmes did take over Martín's responsibilities in the house and send Miss Ross on her way."

I paused to refresh my drink. I had arrived at the point of the story that caused me the most grief, and my throat was going dry. "But there's more, you see. I've finally reached the difficult part, Mr. Lewis—the tragic disaster when Aaron-Smith himself contracted the influenza and died soon thereafter in this very house."

The American fixed me with his penetrating eyes. I could only assume he was incorporating my own experiences into the plans for his novel.

At the time of poor Martín's death," I continued, "Holmes had been here for just a few days. I was still in bed recuperating when he informed me of the devastating news. To my unending sorrow, the more details Holmes provided, the more convinced I became that the young man's death was due to my own wrongdoing."

Lewis raised his hands in protest. "Surely, John, whatever occurred, you're being too hard on yourself."

"No," I said, shaking my head, "I hold myself responsible. When Holmes told me of Martín's passing, I became quite unravelled—still am. In truth, however brief the time I knew him, I had come to regard the young man like a son."

As I spoke to Sinclair Lewis that afternoon, it was close to five years since the tragic event. Yet my eyes began to glisten, and I allowed the whisky to minimize the pain.

Lewis waited a respectful minute before asking, "How well did Sherlock Holmes know Aaron-Smith?"

"Not well at all. They had met upon Holmes's arrival only a few days before Martín's passing. Still, as anyone would conclude who knows the reputation of Sherlock Holmes, a detective like him in the proximity of death—even death from influenza—would set about meticulously examining the conditions surrounding the victim's expiration. In this case, such an examination included the experiments which Martín had been conducting. Let us not forget that Sherlock Holmes is an amateur chemist."

"Right," said Lewis. "I've read *A Study in Scarlet*. According to your account, Holmes was working on a new method for detecting blood stains when the two of you met. Mixing crystals and liquids, taking blood in a pipette."

I smiled at the memory. "You are a thorough reader, Mr. Lewis. He was seeking a faster alternative to the old guaiacum test. 'The most practical medico-legal discovery for years,' he described his work. You may also recall that before we agreed to share a flat, he felt compelled to inform me of his plans to leave chemicals about. Sherlock Holmes, I assure you, knows his way round a laboratory."

"No reason to doubt it. So what did he learn about Aaron-Smith's death?"

"I was still bedridden when Holmes came upstairs from the laboratory to report his findings. Though I was well enough to recall how sombre he looked, the thought of misadventure never crossed my mind. I simply believed him to be disappointed at not having discovered any clues in Martín's notes regarding an antidote to the flu.

"'No immediate cure, eh, Holmes?' I remember asking him with a wry smile.

61

"Yet the furrow in his brow did not disappear. On the contrary, his grave demeanour suggested something else, a grimmer alternative. Soon I came to understand that what caused him such concern was the role he feared I must have played in the tragedy."

Sinclair Lewis pondered this final comment. To my great relief, however, the persistent questioner did not ask me to define just where exactly I fit into the drama. He simply drained his glass and repeated, "Yes, indeed, John. I'd very much like to speak with your friend—if you can arrange it."

Chapter Four

Holmes's Cottage

Microbe hunting is a story of amazing stupidities,
fine intuitions, insane paradoxes.
— Paul de Kruif
Microbe Hunters

*G*lass in hand, Sinclair Lewis stood behind me when I rang Sherlock Holmes. The retired detective had to be summoned from his beehives.

"I can't talk now," Holmes said brusquely when he finally picked up the handset. "Must get back to the apiary. I'm in the midst of preparing sugar syrup."

"Sinclair Lewis, the American writer, wants to meet with you," I told him quickly. "He's got questions about the flu of 1918 for a novel he's writing."

Holmes waited a beat before he repeated my words. "Sinclair Lewis? The Spanish flu?" Pausing long enough for me to contemplate the crackles along the 'phone line, he finally announced, "Lunch. Day after tomorrow. Here."

Then there was silence.

I had rung Sherlock Holmes on Thursday. Mid-Saturday morning Lewis and I met at Victoria Station for our journey to Holmes's cottage in the South Downs.

I first caught sight of the American among the crowd on the platform when, smartly dressed in boater and a bespoke three-piece suit of light-brown tweed, he waved a silver-headed walking stick in my direction. I, in a more commonplace Norfolk jacket, signalled him with my wooden cane.

The down-train would take us through Sussex to the seaside town of Eastbourne. For the excursion, Lewis had brought his ubiquitous notebook and once we had located our seats, began recording his thoughts before we ever began to move. I relied on the *Telegraph* to occupy my time.

Anyone who travels southeast by railway from London to Sussex can testify that not long after the trip begins, the soot-filled city and its smoky environs are replaced by the most beautiful landscape in the world—especially with spring soon to arrive. Indeed, once we entered the countryside, I put down the newspaper to gaze out the window as the train clattered through the pinks and yellows and whites of wildflowers, alongside thick woodlands of dark oak, and up and down the gentle slopes of yellow pastures and green meadows. At varying intervals, congregations of red-brown cattle and thickly-coated sheep would raise their heads and nod as we rushed past.

I had made the trip often enough to recognize the pointed clock tower of the train station as we approached Eastbourne. With a vaulted canopy and lantern roof reminiscent of the famed pavilion some twenty miles to the west, the station's distinctive façade has been described as "Brighton Baroque".

More importantly, I knew where to find the omnibus in nearby Terminus Road that would transport us to the village of Fulworth. Once arrived in Fulworth's High Street, we hired a taxi to motor us the few miles across the South Downs to Holmes's cottage.

The house itself stands on a southern slope near the steep chalk cliffs of Beachy Head, a location from which one can see the silver waves of the Channel and inhale the briny essence of the sea. Beneath a greying sky, I watched a crocodile of young boys follow their school master down the hillocks towards the white cliffs—perhaps for a walk along the Seven Sisters—whilst clamouring gulls circled overhead.

Moments after the taxi had rolled to a halt, Lewis and I crunched our way along the gravel path to Holmes's red front door. Happily, it opened even before we could pull the bell, and Mrs. Hudson emerged with arms outstretched to invite Lewis and me inside. I have written elsewhere how our former landlady at Baker Street had moved to the South Downs many years earlier in order to continue looking after her former tenant.

Sherlock Holmes himself—collarless, in shirtsleeves, and clad in brown, corduroy trousers—trailed close behind. Elsewhere I have also mentioned how I continue to marvel at Holmes's vitality. Whilst I stumble about with a stick and frequently have to cup my hand behind an ear, Holmes—despite the few wisps of grey that streak his hair—seems not to age at all.

Before the three of us could exchange greetings, however, Sinclair Lewis shouted out, "Paul, what on earth are you doing here?"

To my surprise, Holmes was not alone. A tall, burly figure with dark wavy hair strode up behind him. As I was about to learn, standing before us was Paul de Kruif, Lewis's American collaborator on the inchoate novel. "I was invited by Mr. Holmes," he answered his friend.

"But why not tell me you were coming? We're both staying in the Georgian House," Lewis explained, "a swank hotel on Bury Street. You do realize, Paul, that we all could have come down together."

"Mr. Holmes had some work for me to do," de Kruif said cryptically. "He wanted to consult with me before the two of you got here."

Lewis gave a questioning look, but we moved on to introductions. It was just then that Lewis uttered the phrase I had secretly been dreading all the while: "Pleased to meet you, Sherlock."

I froze, gritting my teeth. The only person I had ever heard address my friend by his Christian name was his brother Mycroft.

About to offer his hand to Lewis, Holmes instantly dropped his arm. Beneath cocked bushy brows, he directed at the American as withering a glare with his steel-grey eyes as I have ever seen him deliver.

Sinclair Lewis turned pale, then wilted. "M-Mr. Holmes," he conceded.

The unfortunate matter settled, we followed our host into the dining room where Mrs. Hudson had laid a simple meal of beef sandwiches. In truth, they reminded me of the lunches in Baker Street that Holmes and I used to gobble up before rushing out during an investigation. On this occasion, however, we ate leisurely enough for de Kruif and Lewis to entertain us with some of the highlights of their recently-completed voyage.

"Remember our reconnaissance of Trinidad and Barbados?" de Kruif asked his friend. "Trinidad for shape and—"

"—Barbados for size," said Lewis to complete the thought. Turning to Holmes and me, he explained, "For the new novel, gentlemen, I created a fictional island based on real places. It's where I have the plague break out, and I want the details to be accurate. I call it St. Hubert."

"He makes maps of those fictional places," de Kruif added. "Lots and lots of maps."

"I do for all my work," Lewis explained. "To get things right."

"We were quite something out there," de Kruif laughed, "marching around under pith helmets like British explorers."

"Which we were not," Lewis needlessly pointed out.

"More like a literary safari," de Kruif countered. "We did get a warm reception at the microbe lab in Panama."

"Ah, yes," agreed Lewis. "But don't forget those green-rum swizzles in Barbados—at the Savannah Club in Bridgetown, as I recall."

"And the Planter's Punches at the Ice House in Trinidad," de Kruif reminded him.

Lewis laughed again. "As I always say, gentlemen," he advised Holmes and me, "never fail to drink the wine of the country you're in."

Personally, I could not bring myself to join in the merriment. Given my dark memories of the pandemic—which was, after all, our topic for the day—I considered the jollity out of place.

Holmes may have felt the same, for within a few moments he ended the discussion and indicated that we adjourn to the sitting room.

A fire spluttered in the hearth, and Holmes settled into a deep arm chair with his back to the flames. I took the wing chair next to him; and amid some incidental chatter about the beauty of the neighbouring Downs, de Kruif and Lewis settled themselves on the facing settee.

"Sherry?" Holmes asked.

"Whisky? Lewis countered.

Mrs. Hudson supplied us with our liquid refreshment; and once she left the room, Holmes took the opportunity to light his clay pipe. Lewis in turn produced a package of those Home Run cigarettes he had previously described. I declined the offer though de Kruif joined in, and within minutes we were all enveloped in a miasma of tobacco smoke.

Like a chess player awaiting his opponent's first move, Sherlock Holmes sat placidly eyeing his guests.

An uncomfortable minute or two passed before Sinclair Lewis waved the smoke away as best he could and broached the subject he had come to discuss—the pandemic of 1918 and his novel about a medical hero.

Before he could get beyond "the Spanish flu", however, I interceded. "You need to know," I told Holmes, "that I have already informed Mr. Lewis that the flu is not among my favourite subjects. Regardless of Martín Aaron-Smith's scientific studies, all I ever associate with the pandemic is my inexcusable behaviour related to the young man's death."

"Who's this Aaron-Smith, Mr. Holmes?" de Kruif wanted to know. "You didn't furnish me with any names."

I had no clue as to de Kruif's meaning, but I briefly told him of my young colleague's scientific work and his ultimate death.

"Might I ask," de Kruif said, "the nature of Aaron-Smith's scientific work?"

"Like Dr. Watson," Holmes replied, "I hesitate discussing Aaron-Smith's sad fate. And yet, Professor de Kruif, though it is a subject I too prefer to avoid, it is precisely the reason I took the liberty to engage you, a research scientist familiar with identifying bacteria. In a word, I hope you might be able to shed some light on the affair."

De Kruif opened his mouth—presumably to ask a question.

Holmes held up his hand. "Let me start at the beginning."

Chapter Five

Holmes's Recollection

No more war, no more plague, only the dazed silence
that follows the ceasing of the heavy guns; noiseless
houses with the shades drawn, empty streets,
the dead cold light of tomorrow. . . .
-- Katherine Anne Porter
"Pale Horse, Pale Rider"

*T*hough Sherlock Holmes had directed his gaze at de Kruif, it was Sinclair Lewis who responded. Producing his notebook and pencil, he said to Holmes, "Okay, I'm all ears."

Holmes emitted a sigh, then puffed on his pipe. 'My role in this history began when Aaron-Smith rang me with disturbing news. I remember it as if it were yesterday. 'Dr. Watson's taken ill,' he said. 'He's contracted the flu. He's requested your help.'

"There was never any doubt about my going to the aid of my friend. Understand that for months I had been confined here in my cottage. Mrs. Hudson had arranged with local shops to supply us with food, so we never wanted for staples. I may have been quarantined, but I was quite content. Look round you, gentlemen." Here Holmes waved an arm to encompass his sitting room.

Lewis and de Kruif had seen the room when we had all first entered, of course; but upon invitation they now examined their surroundings with keener interest. I need not explain that the organized clutter was quite familiar to me—the hodgepodge resembled Holmes's aggregation of material that pervaded our former Baker Street digs.

In the main, it was the books that impressed—thousands of them standing in shelves, teetering on tables, and rising from the floor in knee-high stacks. But also demanding attention were the scores of pasteboard storage boxes piled in the four corners of the room. Some were stuffed with ragged-edged papers; others, with cellophane envelopes no doubt containing the remnants of evidence Holmes had collected during various investigations. In the largest boxes, I recognized random memorabilia preserved from any number of Holmes's earliest cases. In one, I saw the small dog-whip that Dr. Roylott had employed to manipulate his swamp adder and in another, the baggy parasol Holmes had carried when disguised as a woman to trail Count Sylvius.

"With so much to occupy my attention," Holmes boasted, "I have never been bored. The quarantine offered me the time to organize my indexes, to study the latest scientific journals, and to complete the monographs I had been planning to write for years. You remember the topics, Watson. The use of dogs in detective work was one and the relationship of typewriters to crime, another. I also got round to penning an introduction to what I plan to be the definitive volume on the art of detection."

"At last," I said approvingly.

"Just what is your central point about the art of detection?" Lewis asked. "That sounds like something worth knowing."

Holmes smiled, exhaling a cloud of smoke. "My 'central point', as you call it, Mr. Lewis, is the importance of logic. To the detective, logic is like a religion. The true detective should be so devout that he will accept no quarter-truths because they are an insult to his faith."

Lewis pointed his pencil at Holmes. "I like that," he said. "I can change it around a bit and use it in the novel." He scribbled the words into his notebook.

"There is always more to do," Holmes added. "Why, I have yet to complete my latest account concerning the role of geometry in the world of bees. Consider the hexagon, gentlemen. According to the ancient mathematician, Pappus of Alexandria, bees somehow know to select just such a geometric figure for their honeycombs."

Lewis had stopped writing at Holmes's mention of geometry and returned to his whisky.

"In some instinctive way," Holmes rattled on, "bees recognize that, given the same total perimeter of the three regular polygons—the square, the triangle, and the hexagon—the hexagon has the largest area and is the only one capable of filling the most space about the same point. In short, gentlemen, bees have somehow reasoned that of the three regular constructs, the hexagon is the most efficient container of honey. The creatures continue to fascinate."

"Marvelous," said de Kruif.

Lewis took a long pull from his glass. "And yet you left all this—all of your unfinished work—to attend Dr. Watson."

Holmes's eyebrows shot up in surprise. "Oh, yes. You see—as Watson will tell you—though a multitude of such preoccupations may fill my days, physical inactivity has always frustrated me. During my professional years, never was I more restless or agitated than when I had no actual cases to pursue."

"Quite right," I put in.

"The prolonged quarantine left me in a similar state," Holmes went on. "Too much confinement during the influenza provided me the lingering opportunity to conjure unsettling visions. Years ago, I would have turned to narcotics to pre-empt such fancies, a behaviour I have long since rejected. But the Spanish flu offered no sympathy, and thus I continually found myself contemplating the ravages of the disease.

"It was as if I could actually feel the physical corruption caused by the illness—the inability to breathe, the constricting horrors of drowning in one's own juices. Worse still, I would conjure the details following my death. I remember contemplating the dimensions of a mass grave dug somewhere in the countryside into which my remains were to be deposited along with those of countless others.

"I can assure you, gentlemen, that in October of '18 when I heard from Aaron-Smith about Watson's illness, I was quite ready to risk liberating myself from quarantine—to stretch my legs, as it were."

I confess that one does not appreciate hearing one's misfortune described as a mere distraction, yet Holmes did eventually add, "As if helping Watson recuperate was not reward enough."

I nodded my appreciation.

"Might I ask for another drink, Mr. Holmes," Lewis said, holding out his glass, "if you'd be so kind."

Holmes put down his pipe and fulfilled Lewis's request. At least by that time, the two Americans had finished smoking their foul-smelling cigarettes.

"It took a day for me to get my things in order," Holmes continued, "primarily to arrange with a neighbour to care for my bees. And then I was off to London."

"Surely not by train," de Kruif said. "Not with the pandemic at its height."

"No, indeed, Professor. I hired a car. Though my research had been limited to newspapers during the quarantine, I still managed to compose a study on the geographic spread of the influenza and learn enough to avoid crowded trains."

"Very wise," said Lewis.

"Surveying the daily prints, I quickly determined the relationship between the disease and our returning soldiers. Mind you, this was prior to the Armistice. The troops arrived at the Channel ports— Dover and Portsmouth, for example—where they took trains to cities like London or Birmingham.

"In London, the Waterloo and Charing Cross stations were the first major stops. It should come as no great surprise then that the boroughs closest to those stations were the ones most immediately infested. The same pattern occurred in smaller cities and towns throughout the country. As such, it was obvious that the railways were places to avoid.

"On Monday, the twenty-first of October, the car arrived at Watson's digs, and I immediately relieved Miss Ross of her responsibilities. That is, I sent her home. Next, I arranged for food to be delivered from the local shops she had listed for me.

As ill as Watson was, there was no problem with keeping him in his bed, and I approached him only when I was wearing a mask.

"Of young Aaron-Smith I saw very little. Recall that I arrived on a Monday, and he died early Thursday morning. During those few days, he continued his daily ministering at Bart's, followed by his work in the laboratory in Watson's basement.

"To be sure, friend Watson's illness was more troubling than what the less-severely infected called the 'three-days' flu'. Yet he seemed to be on the pathway towards recovery. His fever was ebbing, and his coughing fits arrived less frequently."

"I was one of the lucky ones," I said, still able to appreciate my good fortune.

Sherlock Holmes leaned forward in his chair. I understood that the tone of the story was about to grow darker.

"On the fateful Wednesday evening of my first week with Watson," Holmes reported, "Aaron-Smith came home exhausted. He worked for a while in the laboratory; but within the hour, smelling of cigarette smoke, he informed me that his temperature had risen and his breathing had become laboured. I could see that his lips and cheeks were turning a bluish-purple, and I barely managed to get him into his bed."

"The heart leaching oxygen from his blood vessels," said de Kruif. "That's why some people called the Spanish flu the 'Blue Death'."

"Quite so," Holmes replied. "Aaron-Smith himself recognized that his lungs were filling up, and his condition quickly worsened. Soon his entire face was dark, and I knew he was dying. Like a fish out of water, he gasped and writhed. There was nothing I could do, but watch him slowly suffocate in his own fluids. By Thursday morning, he was dead."

Sinclair Lewis had been taking down sentence after sentence; but upon hearing Holmes's last statement, he placed the pencil on an open page and stared back at my friend. As much as the American liked to talk, I realized that he could also be an intense and respectful listener. I believe it is the trait most responsible for the realistic characterizations in his writing.

At the same time, though Sherlock Holmes was looking directly at Lewis and de Kruif, I am convinced he himself was once again envisioning that calamitous night some five years before.

Indeed, a full minute of silence passed before he spoke again. "I rang Bart's to report Aaron-Smith's death and was connected with Dr. Timothy Glass. Strangely, Glass knew that I was staying with Watson; apparently, Aaron-Smith had informed him of the call the young man had made seeking my assistance.

"Assuming that I was the responsible party, Dr. Glass assured me he would notify Aaron-Smith's family in Chipping Norton—his mother, I believe—and send someone round to Queen Anne Street to collect the body. It was a few hours before I heard an ambulance arrive. Two orderlies took charge of the remains. I should tell you that Aaron-Smith was placed in a wooden coffin."

"With caskets at a premium," I reminded everyone, "the young man received more attention than did many another victim."

"Early the following morning," Holmes went on, "I was surprised to receive a note from Dr. Bernard Spilsbury."

"The pathologist," said de Kruif. "I've heard of his work."

"As have I," Lewis reminded us. "The Crippen case."

"Ah, yes," Holmes said, leaning back in his chair and puffing sedately on his pipe, "the Crippen case. In point of fact, Spilsbury and I have worked together on a number of provocative occasions. The sensational press titled our last such affair 'Brides in the Bath'."

"Provocative indeed," said Lewis.

"But off our topic," Holmes reminded the writer.

"Mr. Holmes," Lewis said, "for a plot-seeker like myself, no story is off the topic. What was this one about?"

Holmes shrugged his shoulders. "One George Joseph Smith was charged with drowning three wives in a row. The problem was how in each instance they could be murdered in tubs with very little room. I daresay, one of the women was so large she could not fit her entire person within the bath."

"Yes, yes," said Lewis, his voice rising. "Now that you mention it, I've read of the case. But I never knew that you were involved."

"Not surprising," said Holmes. "Scotland Yard prefer limiting their accolades to members of their own constabulary. Actually, it was not unlike the Crippen inquiry. In this instance, I had been invited to join the investigation by a serious-minded Chief Inspector, Arthur Neil at 'Y' Division.

"To put the matter simply, the Chief Inspector hoped to reconstruct the crimes and asked my opinion of how they might have been committed. Thanks to my knowledge of *baritsu*, I could readily envision the physical manipulations employed by Mr. Smith: with his right hand on the victim's head and his left arm beneath her knees, a sharp uplift of the arm with a simultaneous push down on the head, and the victim instantly slides beneath the water.

"The vagus nerve," I said, instinctively placing my hand on the back of my neck. "The move must take advantage of the vagus nerve that runs from the brain down through the thorax."

"Precisely, Watson. The vagus is highly sensitive to sudden, unexpected attacks, and the rush of water into the nasal passage can have an immediately disabling effect. I assure you, gentlemen, that creating an instant inhibition to the vagal nerve can be quite fatal. Furthermore, a kind of immediate rigor may result, typified by the tightly-clutched soap in the hand of one of the victims. Taken as a whole, Smith's movement was a quick and efficient method of drowning."

"It feels a trifle ghoulish," I said, "to compliment you on reconstructing so macabre a tableau."

Holmes offered a quick smile. "I shared this information with Spilsbury, being careful to warn him not to practice the action on anyone since it can be so immediately effective."

"Quite right," I observed.

"And yet my advice went unheeded. Ever the scientist, Spilsbury shared the theory with the police; and Scotland Yard attempted to replicate the feat with a young woman who volunteered to play the role of victim. Dressed in a bathing costume, she settled into the bath and was pulled underwater with such force that the experiment nearly killed her."

"My God," said Lewis. "You'd have had another murder to investigate."

"Quite so," said Holmes matter-of-factly. "At least, Spilsbury had proved the point. Once he was seen to have got it right, his opinion was deemed irrefutable. Mr. Smith was hanged in Maidstone Prison during the summer of 1915."

"Well," Lewis observed with a dry chuckle, "that took care of that."

"Indeed," Holmes said.

"Which brings us back to the original issue," Lewis went on. "Why would Spilsbury be contacting Sherlock Holmes on the occasion of Aaron-Smith's death?"

Holmes laid down his pipe and steepled his fingers. "A good question. Spilsbury said that Glass had told him that I was responsible for Aaron-Smith's body. I imagine that once Sir Bernard learned that it was I, an erstwhile colleague, who had requested the hospital receive the remains, he regarded it as professional courtesy to let me know he hoped to perform a post-mortem on Aaron-Smith.

"Coincidentally, Spilsbury happened to be in the process of examining the lung and throat tissues of influenza victims for a study he was completing. As was his method in all post-mortems, he recorded his observations on small case-cards. Once he interpreted the data on Aaron-Smith—or so he informed me—the results would comprise part of a report to the Royal Society of Medicine."

"And did you agree?" asked Lewis.

Holmes smiled. "Spilsbury and I have had our disagreements, but this particular endeavour seemed a legitimate request—really, the best way to optimize a sad situation. I granted my approval—such as it was to grant."

De Kruif nodded his own agreement. "So, what were his findings?"

Holmes held up his hand to cut off the question. "In a moment," he said. "More background is required."

Though I had been ill at the time, I did remember that Holmes had communicated with the hospital. I certainly recalled when the morning after Martín had died Holmes went down to the basement to see if he might recover anything of value from Martín's work. Had I been strong enough to stop him, my own pathetic involvement might never have been discovered.

"I hoped to take advantage of the natural light," Holmes continued. "Yet I discovered that in Watson's laboratory there are only a pair of hopper windows on opposite walls. As a result, the basement remains dark during daylight hours. Thanks to Watson's modern thinking, however, the laboratory is, as you may know, equipped with electrical lighting. Once I pushed the button, I could see that the long worktable at the back wall had been set up for two: a pair of microscopes and a pair of Bunsen burners stood at the ready.

"Martín and I worked next to each other," I explained.

"Empty petri dishes, test tubes, beakers, and the like occupied the area between the two workspaces," Holmes said. "Slides and pipettes were stored within easy reach, and a variety of biological specimens filled the vials and flasks on the shelves above."

"We used the area between our two stations to store the materials we shared."

"Indeed," said Holmes. "It all looked quite in order, and yet I was troubled. In the first place, I could find no remnants of Aaron-Smith's work—not even his notes."

"A researcher as careful as he," De Kruif frowned, "would certainly have kept a record of his experiments."

I nodded in agreement. "Sick though I was at the time, I remember Holmes's telling me of his concern. I managed to explain to him how Martín often took his notebooks to Bart's to continue working there. Since I also knew that Martín often shared his findings with Dr. Glass, I assumed that Glass must have been in possession of them just then."

"And yet," Holmes pointed out, "on the shelves above the counter were a number of flasks filled with murky liquids. Obviously, the experiments were not completed."

"Entirely possible," I said. "The upper shelves offered storage for the work we were still conducting—examinations of sputum and lung tissue, for instance. Martín had heard from Glass and Spilsbury about the prominence of pneumococci and streptococci, and we divided our samples along those lines. I worked strictly with the former, Martín with the latter."

"It all sounds pretty regular to me," Lewis said. "Besides not finding any notes, what else was it that troubled you, Mr. Holmes?"

My friend smiled briefly. "You are paying close attention, Mr. Lewis. It is to your credit. You see, there was more to concern me than any missing notebooks. I was drawn to a series of inch-long burns that appeared at irregular intervals at the front-edge of the counter."

"Those were Martín's," I lamented, sensing exactly where Holmes's description was leading. "He insisted on smoking those infernal French cigarettes in our laboratory just he did at Bart's. He'd light them from his Bunsen burner. Sometimes, however, they got in the way of his work, and he would lay them half-smoked at the edge of the counter and let them burn. He did the same in hospital. Most of the time, they burned out. But if there was enough of one left, then later or the next day, when he had finished whatever he'd been working on, he would pick it up and light it again."

"Hard to look into a microscope while smoking, right, John?" Lewis joked.

I did not smile.   Nor did Sherlock Holmes.   On the contrary, darkness shadowed his features once again.

"Most all of the burns were situated at the front-edge of the left-hand side of the counter," Holmes said.

"Martín's side, I pointed out.

"Yet a few of those burns appeared much closer to the area between the two work spaces. More to the point, I could discern through my lens that one of those burns retained a trifling bit of ash. I reckoned that burn to be the most recent since, knowing how important cleanliness is to scientists, I assumed that sooner rather than later the ash would have been swept away."

I remembered this part of Holmes's story—how, when he had returned to my room from the laboratory, he had asked, "You recall my familiarity with tobacco ash, Watson?"

Indeed, I did. Years before, I had read the monograph Holmes had written on the subject. Whilst still suffering from flu, however, I could not then remember its title—*Upon the Distinction Between the Ashes of the Various Tobaccos.*

"'You know my methods, old fellow,' Holmes had said as I lay in bed still groggy with fever. He mentioned something about collecting small flecks of ash from the edge of a table and performing some chemical analyses on them."

"Watson is correct," Holmes said. "I easily identified the French tobacco to which he has already alluded. And yet I also detected something else, some substance alien to smoking-tobacco."

Completely engaged in Holmes's account, Lewis leaned forward. Like a reporter holding his pencil poised to take down the answer, he asked, "What did you find, Mr. Holmes?"

"The residue of active influenza serum," Holmes announced.

"In the tobacco?" Lewis sounded incredulous.

"Enough to kill a regiment," I felt compelled to confess. Nor was I exaggerating. Inhaling the smoke from a cigarette doused with infected serum would be lethal, and remembering Holmes's description of that portentous discovery forced me to prepare myself for the indictment that had to be coming. At any moment, Holmes would report how, on that October morning back in 1918, he had informed me of my own participation in the death of Martín Aaron-Smith.

It was de Kruif who asked the key question. "This serum in the ash—how did it get there?"

Holmes laid out the case. "On a shelf above the cigarette-burn with which we are concerned stood a number of racks containing test-tubes. They were filled with clouded solutions and labelled with the scientific names of various sera. There was also a bowl on the shelf containing a handful of empty test tubes."

"Those were the clean ones we saved for use in new experiments," I explained sadly, well aware of how I was about to be incriminated.

"All of the test tubes in the bowl were empty," Holmes agreed, "save one.   That one was labelled 'Sputum'. It had been left perched at such an angle that though it was closed at its top with a gauze stopper, some of the liquid had seeped through the cloth and dripped down onto the table. It was easy to follow the foot-long trickle across the table-top to the cigarette. A day later— presumably, when Aaron-Smith came upon it—the cigarette would have seemed dry and ready to smoke. Mind, there was only a trace of the stuff, but it was enough."

Lewis bit down on the end of his pencil. "So, what you're saying, Mr. Holmes, is that young Aaron-Smith smoked the contaminated cigarette, and it killed him."

"Precisely," Holmes intoned. "It is the only conclusion that logic will allow."

"Can you go farther?" Lewis persisted. "Just among us friends here, could you tell us whose test tube it was?"

I, of course, knew the answer; it was the singular fact during the pandemic that I hoped never to face. Fortunately, the American's gaze was cast at Holmes and not at me.

Holmes's stolid expression offered no clue. "There was nothing more to learn," he replied coldly.

I understood the reasoning behind the abrupt end to Holmes's investigation. As I have maintained from the start of this narrative, he sought to protect me. Yet during the five years since Martín's death, Lewis's question was the one that continued to resonate. I realized that I could never know for certain who was responsible, and yet I blamed myself. What other answer was there? An old man like me, probably already infected with the influenza, had no doubt left the tube by accident at the precarious angle in a bowl it should not have occupied.

Oh, I suppose a proper barrister could argue that young Martín himself was culpable. Without thinking, Martín could have been the one who mishandled the serum. But I knew him to be more careful than that. With no witnesses to argue the contrary, I laid the blame for the young man's death squarely upon myself.

It was a conclusion I could not escape; and yet to my great surprise, it was also a conclusion that Holmes uncharacteristically had refused to test—

not in October of 1918 and not now before the two Americans five years later. Or so I thought.

Lewis shook his head. "Examining that specimen could have revealed a lot."

In yet another surprise, Paul de Kruif exclaimed, "I'm way ahead of you, Red. That's why Mr. Holmes invited me here. I've already analysed the stuff. I did it in the lab at my flat. You know I've got a microscope and all kinds of other equipment back there."

Lewis and I both stared at de Kruif. Whatever could he mean? What was there left to analyse? Had not the tainted ash been discarded years ago?

Chapter Six

An Alternative Explanation

We hope vaguely, and we dread precisely.
--Paul Valéry
"Disillusionment" (1922)

*S*herlock Holmes held up a newspaper.

"On Tuesday, the sixth of March," he announced, "*The Evening Standard* reported the arrival here in London of Professor Paul de Kruif and Mr. Sinclair Lewis. In fact, their appearance was reported with great enthusiasm."

"Oh, yes," grinned Lewis. "'Spike' Hunt, one of Hearst's boys, met us on the platform at Paddington with a silver shaker full of gin and ice. Most appreciated."

Entertaining, I supposed, but not the sort of story that would have rousted my friend into action.

Holmes tossed the paper aside. "Actually, Watson, it was your decision to come down here with Lewis that started me thinking. Once you rang to arrange the meeting, I reckoned it was finally time to determine the truth about the mysterious cigarette ash. Apparently, I had kept it sealed in a cellophane envelope all these years for just this occasion."

As he spoke, Holmes gestured in the direction of one of his storage boxes; and de Kruif, Lewis and I all turned in unison to look.

"Well aware of de Kruif's proficiency in bacteriology," Holmes continued, "I tracked him down at the Georgian House, and he agreed to analyse the ash. I sent the envelope to him yesterday, along with a telegram inviting him to join us here for lunch today. I did ask him to arrive early, however, so he could share with me the results of his work should I desire—dependent on his findings—to withhold the results even longer."

It is needless to say how much I valued Holmes's motivation.

"Professor," Holmes said to de Kruif, "kindly tell Mr. Lewis and Dr. Watson what you told me."

De Kruif answered before I had time to fully appreciate that for the past five years, I had never considered the possibility that some sort of vindication could ever occur.

"Further analysis of the ash," the microbiologist announced, "revealed a preponderance of pneumococci."

And just like that, just as a wavelet of euphoria was beginning to build, my hopes were dashed. "That proves it then," I said glumly, any thought of redemption now gone. "The pneumococci were in my samples, not Martín's. He was studying streptococci." I shook my head dejectedly. "Try as you might, Holmes, you cannot clear me of this deed."

Sherlock Holmes cocked an eyebrow. "It has been five years since Aaron-Smith's death, Watson. No evidence has ever emerged that indicates you were responsible."

"It was my sample," was all I could say.

"Bunk," Lewis muttered.

Silence descended during which time I suspected that everyone was contemplating the deadly effect of my slipshod work.

At last, Holmes said, "I believe the moment has come, de Kruif, for you to tell what else your experiments uncovered."

"Nothing unusual. Just the fair amount of Pfeiffer's bacillus in the ash not uncommon in such samples."

Had I heard him correctly? "Impossible!" I exclaimed. "You must be in error. Neither I nor Martín ever used samples containing Pfeiffer's. As I've already told Mr. Lewis, despite popular scientific opinion, Martín was convinced that Pfeiffer's was not the cause of the flu. In fact, he believed that doctors were going about inoculating people with ineffectual serum containing the stuff."

"Good man, your friend Aaron-Smith," de Kruif nodded.

"Like some other free-thinkers," I explained, "Martín never feared disagreeing with the so-called experts. The entire point of his work was to seek alternatives to Pfeiffer's. He certainly convinced me. I assure you all that neither one of us ever brought samples containing Pfeiffer's bacillus into our laboratory."

"You told me as much at the time," Holmes said. "That's what makes the professor's conclusion so valuable."

"But, Holmes," I said, "even the noted Dr. Spilsbury thought Pfeiffer's was the agent responsible for influenza."

De Kruif rubbed his chin. "That business troubled me too—how a man with a reputation like his could make so wrong-headed a pronouncement. Then again, I met doctors like him at the Rockefeller Institute. As a result, here's what I believe regarding Spilsbury's conclusion: in order to appear in step with everyone else concerning the importance of Pfeiffer's, he simply relied on the prevailing medical opinion to direct his thinking—however misguided such an opinion might be.

"However wrong, you mean," Lewis pointed out. "If you ask me, this Spilsbury might be worth talking to."

"I already have," said Holmes, "five years ago when he furnished me the results of the post-mortem on Aaron-Smith. That's when he reported he'd found traces of Pfeiffer's bacillus in Aaron-Smith's lungs. He even wrote an article about it."

We all looked at Holmes with curiosity.

"I confess," said he, "that the appearance of Pfeiffer's seemed normal to me. At the time, Watson, I was unaware of your efforts to exclude it. But when I read that de Kruif was in London" – here Holmes nodded at the bacteriologist— "I reasoned that it was the perfect opportunity to get a second opinion on the contents of the ash. As you have just heard, the professor agreed that Pfeiffer's was indeed present in the sample."

"But how can that be?" I demanded.

Once more Sherlock Holmes steepled his long fingers beneath his chin. "Assuming that Spilsbury's original findings were correct, that Pfeiffer's was indeed in Aaron-Smith's lung tissue, we must ask how it got there. I suppose it is possible that the young man inhaled the bacillus at Bart's. And yet, Watson, you yourself have told me that he worked in a laboratory and not with patients. Of course, he might also have become infected with it on his travels beyond the hospital. But given the evidence derived from the ash, I believe it far more likely that Pfeiffer's entered his lungs from the tainted cigarette smoke he inhaled than from anywhere else."

"That is my opinion as well," de Kruif said.

"Do you not see, old fellow?" Holmes said to me. "You are in the clear. If Spilsbury was correct about the bacillus being present in Aaron-Smith's lungs, and you and Aaron-Smith never brought the stuff into your laboratory, then we have to consider another source. We must assume that the test tube containing Pfeiffer's bacillus, the test tube whose contents contaminated the cigarette, was brought into your house by someone else."

"But neither Martín nor I ever brought anyone else into the laboratory," I said.

Lewis's face turned red with excitement. "As a writer who's concocted quite a number of mystery plots, Mr. Holmes, I'm thinking that the 'someone else' you have in mind might have come to Queen Anne Street with evil intent—in short, to murder the young man."

"Quite so," Holmes intoned.

However vague the accusation, the wavelet of euphoria was beginning to grow once more. After five years, I was finally discovering that I might not have been to blame for Martín's death after all.

"About this mysterious other person," Holmes asked me. "Even though you said that the two of you worked alone, might Aaron-Smith have brought someone to your house without your knowledge—perhaps, when you were ill?"

"I can't be sure," I shrugged. "I was delirious half the time—didn't know if it was day or night. Perhaps I heard voices downstairs; perhaps they were in my head. You might ask Miss Ross what she remembers."

"Oh," said Holmes, "I fully intend to do so."

I nodded in agreement. "All I can say for certain is that once I got back on my feet, I disassembled the laboratory in which Martín contracted the influenza. Although the flu continued to rage, I could no longer confront the fateful place. I requested that someone from Bart's come to pick up the Bunsen burners along with the empty flasks and test tubes. No sense in letting them go to waste.

"As for the remaining cultures still growing in agar down there, I asked for those to be taken away as well—with strict instructions for the cultures to be destroyed. Bart's was a safer place for their obliteration than leaving the foul stuff for the dustmen of Queen Anne Street.

"Once the scientific paraphernalia had been removed, I hired a factotum to dismantle the long counter with its tell-tale burn stains. I would have done it myself had my knee allowed me the opportunity. I had the fellow separate the single workspace into its separate components and reposition them in various corners of the basement. In the end, I returned to attending patients at Bart's and, like so many of my colleagues, watched as the awful disease ebbed away the following year."

At the conclusion of my brief but melancholy narrative, Sherlock Holmes rubbed his hands together. "Watson," he announced enthusiastically, "tomorrow is Sunday. I should very much like to interview Miss Ross in Queen Anne Street."

"Fine," I said, surprised at his energy. "But be advised that she attends church in the morning.

"That is not a problem; I have other plans for the morning. Should you wish to join me, I'm hoping to call on Dr. Spilsbury. Perhaps, he can enlighten us further on this business with the bacterium."

"Do come early then," I said. "We can share some toast and jam."

"Capital," Holmes declared, and he relit his pipe, which had gone out during the discussion of Pfeiffer's. "Spilsbury in the morning," he repeated, "Miss Ross in the afternoon."

With Holmes's plan in mind, we adjourned the meeting. Holmes rang for a taxi to convey us back to Fulworth; and Lewis, de Kruif, and I, after offering our good-byes to Holmes and Mrs.

Hudson, awaited the arrival of the motor in front of Holmes's cottage. From Fulworth we made our way back to Eastbourne and caught the late-train up to London.

The journey was a quiet one. Lewis busily wrote in his notebook, and de Kruif closed his eyes and let the railway rock him to sleep. I stared out into the encroaching darkness, daring to re-evaluate what for years I had thought of as my culpatory role in the death of Martín Aaron-Smith.

Despite the lateness of our arrival in London, the railway platform at Victoria was full of travellers—in great contrast, I noted, to those days of flu when most of the trains were at a standstill.

The three of us shared a taxi that stopped first in Bury Street before Georgian House. Lewis and De Kruif exited the cab; but as Lewis was walking off, he turned round and motioned for me to open the window so he could add a final word.

"For all your help, John," he said, "I'll be sure to drop a reference or two about your friend Sherlock Holmes into the new novel. Who knows?" he winked. "I might even have a character read some of the Holmes adventures that you yourself have written." With a farewell wave he re-joined de Kruif, and together they entered the massive block of red-brick.

I allowed myself a self-indulgent smile before addressing the driver: "Queen Anne Street, if you please."

Chapter Seven

Sir Bernard

I have never claimed to be God—
but merely his *locum* on his weekends off.
--Sir Bernard Spilsbury
Quoted by Andrew Rose
In *Lethal Witness*

*A*t eleven o'clock Sunday morning in the middle of a thin rain, Sherlock Holmes arrived in Queen Anne Street. He joined me at table; and as I had promised, we shared toast and an assortment of the jams Miss Ross had left for me.

"You recall our destination?" Holmes asked over coffee.

"Of course," I said. "31 Marlborough Hill in St. John's Wood. Most medical people even remotely connected with the world of forensics know the address of the Honorary Pathologist of the Home Office."

"Indeed, Watson," said Holmes sipping his coffee, "and this being Sunday, I expect Sir Bernard to be at that location. Yet according to my sources at the Home Office, what many in the 'world of forensics'—let alone the rest of society—do not know is that Spilsbury has also rented a top-floor flat at 1 Verulam Buildings in Gray's Inn—a flat, I might add, equipped with a laboratory."

"Gray's Inn? Why the need?"

"I should imagine he has his personal reasons for escaping from his wife and four children. He can live in Gray's Inn on his own terms, conduct his own experiments, and, of course, entertain whomever he chooses. It should be noted that he has taken on as his assistant, one Hilda Bainbridge, the widow of a former associate. She joined him not long after the death of her husband."

"Bainbridge," I said to myself. "Could you be referring to Francis Bainbridge, the medical professor?"

"Quite so."

"Why, I knew Bainbridge at Bart's. Chair of physiology, if I remember correctly. Decent chap. Captain in the Royal Army Medical Corps. Liked to hike about in the hills, as I recall. But see here, Holmes, Spilsbury is beyond reproach. I am sure that Mrs. Bainbridge has joined him in a purely professional capacity."

Holmes refused to be drawn into idle speculation, "Whatever the case," he replied, "Spilsbury returns to Marlborough Hill for lunch every Sunday, so at this moment we know where to find him."

There had been a time when, despite the rain, I might have suggested to Holmes that we walk the two-and-a-half miles to north London. After all, part of the route traverses the splendid gardens of Regent's Park. But in these later years, with my knee no longer cooperating, we hired a cab, skirted the park, and soon enough were deposited in St. John's Wood before Sir Bernard's large, semi-detached, three-storey house of light-yellow brick.

Exiting the taxi, we opened our umbrellas. "With all the man's successes," I observed, staring up at the house, "I shouldn't wonder to see a blue plaque on the wall someday."

Beyond cocking a sceptical eyebrow, Holmes failed to respond. Instead, he marched forward to the outer door, paused, and proceeded to ring the electric bell.

Minutes passed, and the rain beat harder. Holmes rang again.

At last, the door opened a crack. In spite of the curtain of gloom and rain outside, there remained enough light to reflect off a pair of round, black-rimmed, spectacles peering at us from a darkened interior. Behind the glasses, which I did not remember from a few years before, I could barely discern the chiselled face of Sir Bernard. It took him a moment to recognize Sherlock Holmes; but when he did, he reluctantly opened the door wider.

The pathologist wore a long white apron mottled with mud-red drips and dull-yellow smears of varying intensities. His shirtsleeves were devoid of cuffs whilst an orange rubber glove encased his right hand. One needed no great powers of deduction to conclude that the house, like Spilsbury's flat in Gray's Inn, contained a personal laboratory. Equally obvious was the fact that we had disturbed the great man at his work.

"Sherlock Holmes," the pathologist muttered. No smile accompanied this response nor, I might add, an invitation to come in out of the wet. "This seems to be the day for visitors," he announced, his voice stronger.

"Who else has come by, if you don't mind my asking?" Holmes said, heavy droplets thudding atop our umbrellas.

"Two Americans," Spilsbury said loud enough to be heard over the rain, "a ginger-haired writer and a rather large person who claimed to be a bacteriologist. If you can believe it, Holmes, they were asking me questions about ancient history—the Spanish flu. The writer said it had something to do with a book he was putting together."

Clearly, Sinclair Lewis and Paul de Kruif had interviewed Dr. Spilsbury before we had the opportunity; simply put, they had appropriated Holmes's plan.

Yet my friend appeared unflustered. Instead, he said with a slight bow of his head, "Sir Bernard, this is my friend and colleague, Dr. John Watson."

"Doctor," he said.

"Doctor," I replied awkwardly, then added, "we met briefly in Bart's a few years ago. Actually, it was during the pandemic you just mentioned."

Spilsbury bristled, obviously not the sort who enjoyed being informed he had forgotten having met someone. "Sorry," he said. "I was inundated with corpses in those days. I suppose I still am," he chuckled wryly as he turned to Holmes.

Suddenly, he looked back at me. "Watson," he said, 'Watson of Queen Anne Street?"

"Why, yes," I answered, raising my umbrella so he could get a better look at me. At the same time, I wondered how, if he did not remember me from Bart's, he none the less knew where I lived.

Holmes, however, had other issues in mind. "Dr. Watson and I have a few questions we'd like to ask you."

"Out of retirement again, eh, Holmes?"

My friend smiled. "No, Sir Bernard, just a few reminiscences about the Spanish flu."

"You as well?" the pathologist frowned. "Like a magnet, that pandemic continues to attract. First, the Americans, now the two of you. I really don't have the time for this. My family is out, and I'm in the middle of some work—though, actually, Holmes, it's just the sort of thing in which a detective like yourself might be interested. I've been studying the effects of putrefaction on bruises. I'm trying to determine if, over time, the bruises on a corpse disappear and thus eliminate tell-tale signs of trauma."

"As best I remember," I felt obliged to put in, "they may actually darken as the skin putrefies."

Sir Bernard Spilsbury looked at me with what I can only describe as a sympathetic smirk.

"Yes, quite, Doctor," he said, rendering hollow the title of which I have always been so proud.

Holmes took a step forward to intervene. "We won't be long, Sir Bernard."

With another frown, the pathologist backed up a pace and then reluctantly ushered us into the darkened entry hall. Rather than the upright posture I remembered from our first meeting, Sir Bernard now seemed to stoop; and behind his glasses, I noted lines beneath his eyes that I had not seen before. He did have the presence of mind to put our brollies into an umbrella stand and to take our wet coats and hats before leading us toward an austere but brighter sitting room.

Sir Bernard struggled to pull off the rubber glove and, when he had succeeded, reached for a cigarette package on a side table. After offering us smokes, which we declined, he proceeded to strike a match and light a cigarette. It was rumoured he smoked fifty a day. Though the pathologist was widely known for quite literally sniffing out clues from the malodorous corpses he opened, some of his colleagues believed that Spilsbury relied on the cigarette smoke to cover the stench of death. Others feared the opposite—that the cigarettes were interfering with his sense of smell.

Sir Bernard remained in his white apron throughout our conversation—no doubt with the intention of encouraging our speedy exit. Atop a nearby mahogany *escritoire* lay a small pile of three-by-four-inch case-cards filled with a cribbed, left-slanting script—presumably, the celebrated notes he made during the thousands of post-mortems he had completed.

"You may recall, Sir Bernard," Holmes began, "that you performed an autopsy on a young scientist who worked at Bart's in 1918—one Martín Aaron-Smith. I was the person responsible for the remains."

Sir Bernard exhaled a cloud of smoke before speaking. "Now that does sound familiar. I believe it was Glass who informed me of your role at the time."

"Perhaps," I added, "you had the occasion to meet Aaron-Smith at Bart's since you both worked there."

The pathologist stroked his square jaw. "That goes back a few years. I was quite busy during the pandemic. One had to be prepared for duty twenty-four hours a day—four thousand dead per week, if you recall. And yet, as you say, Watson, I might have had the occasion to meet him."

"This is more about your research than the autopsies, Sir Bernard," Holmes said. "Aaron-Smith was a microbiologist who rejected the bacillus called Pfeiffer's as the origin of the influenza. Rather than speculating about bacteria that he felt were not the cause of the disease, he spent most of his free time in hopes of discovering the true catalyst."

"And what is that to me?" the pathologist asked amid another exhalation of smoke.

Holmes offered a quick smile. "Within most medical circles, Sir Bernard, your word is highly prized. And yet you strongly endorsed the unproven proposition that Pfeiffer's bacterium was the cause of the Spanish flu."

Sir Bernard nodded slowly. "Indeed, I wrote an article to that effect."

"Yes, you did," Holmes said. "In fact, the body of Aaron-Smith was one of the flu's victims you studied."

"Is that so?" Spilsbury asked. "I don't recall. But if that is the case, Watson," he laughed cynically, "one must assume you were correct when you suggested that I had actually met the fellow."

It took all my self-control not to call out Sir Bernard's coldness in the face of Martín's death.

Unmoved, the pathologist held up a forefinger, signalling us to wait a moment. He then got to his feet and, laying his cigarette in a glass ashtray next to the case-cards, proceeded to open the hinged top of the *escritoire* and withdraw from an inner shelf a few sheets of paper.

"The article itself, gentlemen," he announced with a brief wave of the pages "from the *Journal of the Royal Society of Medicine,* November 1919.

"I based my conclusions," Spilsbury said as he retrieved his cigarette and regained his seat, "upon the post-mortems of twenty souls who had recently died, a combination of male and female adults and infants. You say this Aaron-Smith was one." With an unsympathetic shrug, he proceeded to read aloud, 'The most constant morbid condition was acute inflammation of the air passages. It was the vivid, "flaming" variety with abundant purulent exudate in the upper air passages.'"

Following the technical description, Sir Bernard set down the pages. "It was in a majority of these specimens," he announced, "that in addition to pneumococci and streptococci, I discovered *H. influenzae*—Pfeiffer's bacillus, as you have termed it."

"In what percentage of your cases did you find such evidence?" my friend asked. Well aware of the article in question, Holmes clearly knew the answer to his query.

"About sixty percent."

Holmes shook his head. "Come now, Sir Bernard. As you yourself must acknowledge, sixty percent is hardly persuasive. I can only wonder what led you to so definitive a conclusion based on such tenuous evidence."

Sir Bernard's jaw tightened. I am certain he was not used to being prodded. "As I explained in the article"—he picked up the pages in order to cite his response exactly as he had written it— "either 'my search was not sufficiently thorough or the organism had disappeared before death.'"

"'Not sufficiently thorough'? Holmes questioned. 'Disappeared before death'? Hardly a convincing argument."

"Nonetheless, Mr. Holmes, it was what I believed at the time—and what I still believe today." The pathologist breathed deeply. I am also certain he was not used to being contradicted.

At this point, I should add that even now, well after 1918, Spilsbury's steadfast attitude has continued to cause distraction. Just the previous year, my literary agent, Conan Doyle—widely recognized for investigating criminal cases on his own—took exception to Sir Bernard's obvious sense of self-assurance. Sir Arthur suggested that Spilsbury should be embarrassed by the infallibility that juries ascribe to him—too much power in the hands of a single man.[*] It is a rigidity that certainly helps explain the sway that Spilsbury's less-than-persuasive view of Pfeiffer's bacillus had on others.

"Glass at Bart's concurred," Sir Bernard maintained. "He assured me that the bacillus was the cause—the 'aetiology', his word—of the flu. He told me that all the doctors at Bart's were in agreement."

"In agreement with the less-than-convincing sixty percent in your findings?" Holmes persisted. "Come now, Sir Bernard."

The pathologist removed his glasses and rubbed his eyes. "I'll be honest with you, gentlemen," said he, shaking his head. "I was facing significant pressure at the time. As far back as 1918, I suspected a knighthood might be in my future, and I did not care to upset the thinking in Downing Street. I wanted matters to go smoothly, and so I sided with the conventional opinion furnished to me by Dr. Glass— an opinion, which, of course, I still favour."

"But as a doctor, Sir Bernard," I demanded, "how could you express an opinion not strongly supported by your own findings?"

"I stand by my conclusions, Doctor," Spilsbury said more forcefully this time. "Despite the

---

[*] Conan Doyle's doubts are reported in the *Evening Standard*, 20 April 1925.

prattle of the so-called 'anti-Pfeiffer's school', they have never conclusively disproven that Pfeiffer's was the cause of the Spanish flu."

Sir Bernard Spilsbury was a principled man, but he was also a stubborn one. Clearly, he wanted to be on the winning side—in this case, that of the believers in Pfeiffer's—even if it meant admitting a short-coming in the effectiveness of his own procedures.

"Gentlemen," Sir Bernard said, replacing his glasses as he rose, "I fear I've taken enough time from my work." He snuffed out the cigarette in the ashtray before concluding, "I must return to my laboratory upstairs. If you'll excuse me?"

He raised his arm in the direction of the entry hall, and Holmes and I made our way towards the door.

"Ask Dr. Glass," the pathologist said as he handed us our umbrellas and coats. "He supported Pfeiffer's as well."

By the time we left Sir Bernard's house, the fierce rain had transformed into a soft drizzle. We hailed a taxi; and as we motored back to Queen Anne Street, I could not help wondering about Sir Bernard's thinking. "How can a man of Spilsbury's distinction defend his own suspect work simply to remain on the popular side of a scientific proposition?"

"The man has a paradoxical reputation," said Holmes. "Among the police and the courts, he has earned the highest accolades. But among his immediate colleagues—medical men and academics—he commands little distinction. His standings within both groups help explain his decision about the bacillus."

"Trying to bridge two camps," I suggested.

But Holmes was no longer listening. Soon we would be questioning our next witness, and I was certain that just then he was contemplating what he wanted to ask my housekeeper. Unlike our exchanges with Dr. Spilsbury, whose ideas figured so prominently in Holmes's investigation, I could not imagine what thoughts Miss Ross might have that would shed additional light on his concerns.

Chapter Eight

Star-Crossed

What's true of all the evils in the world is true of plague
as well. It helps men to rise above themselves.
— Albert Camus
The Plague

*H*yacinth Ross began working for me
after Christmas in 1917. At that time, she still lived
with her parents in Camden Town—not too far, in
fact, from the notorious Hilldrop Crescent address of
Dr. Crippen. I had learned of her availability from our
own Mrs. Hudson, who, as it turned out, had been a
good friend of Miss Ross's mother for many years.

After my wife's passing, Miss Ross was
all I could have hoped for in a housekeeper. When I
became ill in October of 1918, she actually moved
into my house to care for me. In some singular
manner, the arrival of Miss Ross created a sense of
extended family.

It was with only a vague hope of gaining
fresh information concerning Aaron-Smith's death
that Holmes and I awaited Miss Ross's arrival. As the
afternoon wore on, the sky darkened, and the rain

showers resumed. Sherlock Holmes took it upon himself to set a fire in the hearth.

Near four o'clock Holmes informed me that he had heard the latch to the rear entrance release, thus announcing the arrival of the housekeeper. I immediately rose to tell the young woman of our desire to speak with her.

When I greeted Miss Ross, she was carefully hooking her slick, dark-blue trench-coat—so named because of its similarity to the military outer wear worn in the trenches during the Great War—upon a peg in the passageway beyond the kitchen.

As usual, Miss Ross was dressed in black; yet despite the weather and her dark clothing, her demeanour was anything but dour. She had known Sherlock Holmes from the days of the flu; and whilst the overly critical might question whether she held a grudge against him for having sent her home during the pandemic, Miss Ross regarded Holmes a hero for having come all the way to London to care for his good friend.

No sooner did I inform her that Holmes wished to ask her a few questions than she insisted upon making us tea.

"I'll bring it right in, Doctor. Then I'll be happy to speak with the gentleman."

"We'll be waiting in the dining room," I told her.

Miss Ross joined us a few minutes later, a white apron tied at her waist, the tray in her hands laden with the *accoutrements* for tea including my favourite chocolate biscuits. She placed the white-porcelain tea pot, cups and biscuit-plates on the table, but obviously misunderstanding her own role in the repast, had laid settings for just Holmes and me.

"You are to join us, Miss Ross," I reminded her, appropriating an additional cup and saucer from amongst the china on the cherrywood sideboard.

"I understand your request, sir," she said, "but you must first allow me to pour the tea."

Only after placing the newly-filled cups before Holmes and me, did she sit down and take the cup I had provided for her.

"Strong Darjeeling," I said to Holmes, "with a bit of Lapsang Souchong, just the way you like it."

He leaned forward and inhaled the smoky aroma, then took a sip and smiled at the housekeeper.

"Now, Miss Ross," I said, judging her preparations to have been completed, "all that we are about to ask you is related to the visit last Thursday of that rather strange American writer. You remember; you opened the door for him."

"The man with the red hair," she nodded.

Sherlock Holmes leaned forward. "Yes, the man with the red hair. But what we really would like to know goes back much further. Hard as it may be, please recall if you can those dark days of the Spanish flu when you were attending Dr. Watson."

She shook her head. "Days I'd like to forget—with all due respect, Mr. Holmes, having met you at the time."

"Just so," murmured Holmes. "But you do remember Martín Aaron-Smith, the young scientist who stayed here for a number of weeks. He worked with Dr Watson in the laboratory downstairs."

Strange to say, at Holmes's mention of Martín's name, a change occurred in Miss Ross's demeanour. She shifted restlessly in her chair, and with a blush colouring her face, flashed a conflicting mix of emotions. A smile crossed her lips undercut immediately by a sadness that filled her eyes. "A handsome young man," she remembered. "I was so sorry when I learnt of his passing."

"Did you speak to him much?" I asked. "Perhaps when I was ill?"

"Yes, Doctor," she said, staring down into her tea. "The week before Mr. Holmes arrived and sent me off, you might say that Mr. Aaron-Smith—Martín—and I spent some time getting to know one another."

This development was, of course, new to me.

Holmes cocked an eyebrow at her admission. "Could you elaborate further."

Miss Ross offered a wistful smile. "Even before I came to stay, I knew that Martín and Dr. Watson worked together in the laboratory. During the week I was here after Dr. Watson took ill, Martín continued on his own down there." She paused a moment to drink her tea. I think it also provided her the chance to savour her memories.

"I would stand at the top of the stairs and watch him. He smoked those horrible cigarettes and then mixed his strange brews in the glass tubes. He never looked my way. When he was at work, there was nothing that could distract him."

"Quite correct," I said.

"But one night after Dr. Watson first became ill, Martín said he needed a change of scenery and came into the kitchen. He had no one to talk with, you see. He would complain to me of his tedious work at St. Bart's—how depressing a place it was with all the sick and dying people. Then he'd turn round and speak of his hopes for finding some remedy, some antidote, some sort of medicine, that might end the horrible flu. We shared the odd cuppa together, and one evening before Mr. Holmes arrived, Martín suggested we sit in the garden together. We did so a few times when you were sleeping, Dr. Watson."

This part of the story was also new to me.

"We would take off our masks and enjoy the evening air. I'd like to think I offered him an opportunity to feel at ease. One night there was a severe chill, and he gave me his coat to wear."

"Quite the *gallant*," I found myself thinking.

"He told me about growing up in the Cotswolds," Miss Ross continued, "and how he used to run up and down the hills in the countryside when he was a lad. He spoke of his years in Oxford where he read biology at Pembroke. He went on about his fascination with science and tried to explain subjects I didn't understand. But then he would stop and ask me questions about my own family and my work here for you, Dr. Watson."

Quite the young gentleman I took him to be.

"Martín told me that if it weren't for the flu, he would like to escort me to the cinema and to dinner." She picked at the corners of the napkin in her lap. Then she said, "I would be lying to you, gentlemen, if I didn't admit to thinking of spending my future with him." Here she blushed again. "But, of course," she whispered, "that was not to be," and then she fell silent.

Whilst simultaneously enlightening, provocative, and melancholy, Miss Ross's nostalgic recollections had so far addressed none of the questions Holmes wanted answered. As a consequence, his next query was more direct. "During the week you were here when Dr. Watson was ill, Miss Ross, do you recall if Aaron-Smith had any visitors?"

Miss Ross sat up straighter and bit her lip as, eyes narrowing, she moved to a new area of her memory. "Now that you bring it up, sir, I do remember something of the sort. It seemed strange to me at the time because it was so unusual. Martín had never brought anyone to the house before.

"Two gentlemen they were who visited here on separate occasions. Both doctors, I believe, from St. Bart's—though I don't recall their names. The first time—I think it was a Friday night—the one came by himself; the next time—I remember because it was the evening before you arrived, Mr. Holmes—there were the two, as I said. Quite distinctive they were."

Holmes's eyes flashed as he sensed his prey. "In what manner? What was it that made them so distinctive?"

"Distinctive in their appearance, I mean. One of the gentlemen wore a black eye-patch. The other was quite fashionably dressed."

"Which of the two—"

"Glass and Spilsbury," I interrupted. "No wonder that Spilsbury knew of my house when we spoke earlier."

Holmes frowned.

I had upset the rhythm of his questioning, and I knew well enough to return to my tea.

"Which of the two," he repeated, "came twice?"

"The gentleman with the eye-patch."

"Do you remember the nature of the visits?" Holmes asked. "It would be most helpful if you could."

Miss Ross shook her head. "That I'm sorry I can't tell you, sir, though I do remember something strange. On the first occasion, the one gentleman with the eye-patch arrived with Mr. Aaron-Smith, and Martín was about to lead him downstairs to the laboratory. But the man with the eye-patch insisted on speaking to me."

"Curious," muttered Holmes. "What did he have to say?"

"He told me he was a doctor who worked with Martín in hospital, and he asked about my health. With everyone so sick with flu, it seemed quite a sensible question at the time. Then for some reason, he began asking about my duties here and how I liked my work. Only after I answered his questions did he follow Martín downstairs."

"No doubt establishing his identity with you," Holmes said. "Pray, continue, Miss Ross."

"I heard some words pass between him and Martín in the laboratory, but couldn't make them out. Soon thereafter, Martín came up for two glasses of port. I told him I would bring them down, but he said he would take them himself. I heard nothing else and soon went off to the room Dr. Watson had provided me."

I picked up a biscuit whilst Sherlock Holmes drummed the fingers of his right hand on the table top. "And the second visit—the night before I arrived?"

"That was Sunday—I remember now. The man with the eye-patch arrived with the well-dressed gentleman, as I have said."

"And Martín?" Holmes asked.

"Oh, he was not with them."

I swallowed the entire biscuit on that bit of news.

Miss Ross noticed my reaction. "I was quite surprised myself, Dr. Watson. But the gentleman with the eye-patch set me at ease. I knew him from his first visit, after all. He told me that Martín had needed something from his laboratory here; and since Martín was working late at St. Bart's, he had asked the gentleman to get it for him."

"And the well-dressed fellow?"

"Oh, he spoke to me for the few minutes the other gentleman was downstairs. He was a bit cold, I have to admit—but refined, don't you know? And very good-looking if I am permitted to say so."

"Spilsbury to a T," I observed.

"Did the man with the eye-patch find what he had been looking for downstairs?" Holmes asked.

"If he did, sir, he never shared the information with me."

Holmes got to his feet. "Miss Ross," he said, "You have been most helpful indeed. Come, Watson, there is still more to discuss."

"Feel free to finish your tea," I told Miss Ross as I followed Holmes into the sitting room.

No sooner were we gone from the table, however, than Miss Ross collected the dishes and glassware on the tray and retired to the kitchen.

Sherlock Holmes stoked the fire and then joined me in front of the hearth.

"On the first visit," Holmes said, "Glass came here with Aaron-Smith to meet Miss Ross. Glass spoke to her at length so she would know him when he came again. That much seems evident. On the evening of the second visit, he had doubtlessly provided Aaron-Smith with extra work so the young man wouldn't be here to interfere with Glass's plans. Once Aaron-Smith had informed Glass that I was to arrive on Monday, it made imperative Glass's visit here Sunday night."

"And Spilsbury?" I asked.

"I'm certain he brought Spilsbury along to distract Miss Ross whilst Glass attended to matters downstairs in the laboratory. I doubt Spilsbury had any knowledge of what Glass was about." Holmes narrowed his eyes as he said, "I also doubt that Glass was truly searching for something that Aaron-Smith had requested. Whatever the true nature of Glass's activities in the laboratory that night I hope to discover from the man himself."

I recognized the edge in my friend's voice; it is the icy tone he employs when he suspects foul play.

Sherlock Holmes might have been reading my mind when he next spoke. "As I have said before, old fellow, 'When a doctor goes wrong, he is the first of criminals.'"

Chapter Nine

Questions Answered

And Darkness and Decay and the Red Death
held illimitable dominion over all.
--Edgar Allan Poe
"The Mask of the Red Death"

*M*onday morning during coffee, I examined the most recent medical register in search of the current whereabouts of Dr. Timothy Glass. Sherlock Holmes confined his own activities to perusing the prints.

"I say, Holmes," I announced a few moments later, "though Glass still maintains a professional relationship with Bart's, he has a surgery close by in Harley Street. He's been working there for the past three years."

"Harley Street," Holmes mused. "One's medical practice has to be quite successful to afford the upkeep of an office in such surroundings."

"Or know the proper people," I said, before drinking my coffee.

Harley Street, less than a mile from my own abode, epitomized the so-called Doctors' quarters of London. A century earlier, the neighbourhood of Georgian-styled houses had begun attracting members of the medical profession, and the surrounding area had slowly evolved into London's most lucrative centre for medicos as well as for scientific professionals with connections to them. I lived on the outskirts.

A 'phone call to the Harley Street surgery of Dr. Glass assured us that whilst the doctor was not in at present, he would be in attendance later that afternoon.

For the next three hours, Holmes and I busied ourselves reading newspapers and other assorted periodicals. At last, after a final coffee, we undertook the short walk to the office of Dr. Glass, I employing my stick to match the long strides of my friend.

It was a fine day for a stroll in spite of the roar of motors and the braying of horns. Beneath an array of white clouds scudding across a rich blue sky, Holmes and I headed east on Queen Anne Street, turning south into Harley where the plane trees of Cavendish Square marked the end of the road.

The walk took but a few minutes, and we soon discovered the town house whose open iron gate bore the shiny brass plaque reading *Mr. Timothy Glass, M.D.* I paused for a moment not only to admire the signage but also to give my knee a rest. Yet when I started to move again, I immediately felt Holmes's hand on my arm and saw him nod in the direction of the dark-blue double-doors at the entry.

I stopped short. To my amazement, a pair of familiar figures were just then exiting, one of them wearing a tweed flat cap and wrapped in a long black cape, the other sporting a black beret. It was the Americans, of course, Sinclair Lewis and Paul De Kruif.

Upon seeing the two of us, Lewis instinctively mirrored my friend. He touched de Kruif on the arm and flicked his head in our direction. Like me, de Kruif stopped short in surprise. The writer turned as if to leave, but Holmes deprived him of the opportunity.

"What have you told Glass?" Holmes demanded of Lewis even before reaching him.

"Not a very pleasant way to greet a fellow," the American replied, his red face unusually pale, the scar on his cheek glowing white.

"Enough," commanded Holmes. "We know that you talked with Spilsbury yesterday morning."

"That's right," said de Kruif, "we did."

"Would you believe," Lewis added, "that Spilsbury actually told us that he'd relied on Glass's advice to justify his conclusion about Pfeiffer's—to confirm it as the cause of the flu?"

"Spilsbury told us much the same," said Holmes. "The significant question is how much of what Spilsbury said did you relate to Glass just now?"

"All of it," Lewis smiled, his face regaining its reddish hue. "We told Glass how Spilsbury said he'd depended on Glass for guidance; how thanks to Glass—not to mention some shaky research of his own—Spilsbury wrongly named Pfeiffer's bacillus the cause of the Spanish flu."

"You told him nothing more?" Holmes questioned, the knuckles of both hands turning white. "Nothing about Spilsbury's visit with Glass to Queen Anne Street on a Sunday night in October of '18? Nothing about the tainted cigarette?"

Lewis removed his cap and ran his fingers through his red hair. "I don't know what you're talking about. John here told us about the cigarette. I had no idea that Spilsbury was connected to it."

"I don't think he is," answered Holmes. "I don't believe Sir Bernard knew what Glass was doing in the laboratory when Sir Bernard accompanied him to Watson's house. I believe that Sir Bernard was there simply to distract the housekeeper."

Lewis looked confused.

"I didn't know either one of them had been to Watson's lab," said de Kruif. Turning to Lewis, he added, "Wait a minute, Red. Didn't you just tell Glass that Mr. Holmes's plan was to speak to the housekeeper after their visit with Spilsbury?"

Sinclair Lewis's red face paled again. "I may have mentioned something of the sort to Dr. Glass. But nothing else." He brushed his hands together as if to wash away any further discussion of the matter.

Holmes took a deep breath. "Gentlemen, Dr. Glass is a smart man. If he learned from you that I spoke with the housekeeper, he will no doubt realize that I will be able to reconstruct the true facts concerning the death of Martín Aaron-Smith at Queen Anne Street."

"And just what are those facts?" Lewis wanted to know.

Sherlock Holmes spoke quickly—in exasperation, it seemed to me. "To begin with, there's the fact that Glass arranged for Sir Bernard to keep the housekeeper occupied whilst Glass went down to the laboratory. There's also the fact that Glass found the partially-smoked cigarette, which Aaron-Smith had left on the counter—a habit, Watson has assured me—the young man used to do at Bart's.

"Just what are you suggesting, Mr. Holmes?" asked de Kruif.

"What I am suggesting is that Dr. Timothy Glass produced a vial which he must have brought on his person to Watson's laboratory, found the extinguished cigarette he hoped would be there on the work table, and doused it with the tainted serum. It would take little effort to then dribble a line of the stuff back towards the shelf and place the test tube at a dangerous angle in the container above the dribble. In such a manner, it would appear that the serum had dripped naturally onto the table top and into the tobacco. Had there been no such cigarette, I imagine Glass would have found some other equally nefarious method for exposing Aaron-Smith to the serum."

"But why, Holmes?" I asked.

"I am no reader of minds," Holmes said, "but I must assume that Glass's career was inextricably bound to that of Sir Bernard's. By identifying Pfeiffer's as the cause of the Spanish flu, Glass helped establish the reputation of Spilsbury. At the same time, recall that Spilsbury's post-mortem studies conveniently re-enforced Glass's pronouncement."

"A perfect example," Lewis proclaimed, "of the old German proverb, *'Eine Hand wäscht die andere.'*"

"Quite so," said Holmes. "Had Aaron-Smith been successful in undermining Glass's faith in Pfeiffer's, he would have been discrediting Spilsbury's work at the same time. Such a calamity would certainly have caused Glass's career to come tumbling down."

"And ended any chance of Spilsbury's presumed knighthood," I added.

Sinclair Lewis shook his head. "I didn't tell Dr. Glass any of this, Mr. Holmes, simply because I didn't know any of it."

"None the less, from what you have already told him, Lewis, Glass will realize the game is over. We must—"

Suddenly, a gunshot rang out. Even with my impaired hearing I could tell it came from inside the medical building, and we all turned in the direction of Glass's surgery. De Kruif was the first to rush towards the office, and immediately we all followed.

The blue outer doors were unlatched, as was the door to Glass's waiting room. The room itself was empty, and no one was seated at the nurse's station by the entrance to Glass's personal office. He must have turned everyone out.

Holmes knocked loudly on the door, but received no reply. He knocked louder still and again received no answer.

Though Holmes and I had not worked together lately, there are certain communications between long-time comrades that neither one ever forgets. The two of us exchanged glances, responded with a nod, and were about to put our shoulders to the door without a word being spoken. In preparation, I hung the curved wooden handle of my cane over my forearm ready to give my all to our endeavour.

Fortunately, the much younger and larger De Kruif interceded. One of his determined shoulders broke the door open with a crash.

Holmes slipped in first and held the rest of us back. Even so, we could see past him and through the doorway.

It was the familiarity of the scene that made it so particularly chilling—a doctor's office, albeit a fashionable one. The surroundings were eerily recognizable: the red-leather turning chair behind the shiny mahogany desk; the black leather chairs opposite; the leather-bound anatomy books standing in a wall of oak shelves; and lying on a steel tray atop a table a few feet to the right, various pieces of medical equipment—a binaural stethoscope, a mercury thermometer, and a Queen Square reflex hammer with a bamboo handle.

Disrupting the familiarity, however, was the body of the man I recognized as Doctor Timothy Glass. He was slumped forward across the desktop, a Webley pistol lying on the floor by his right hand, which hung limply by his side. His head rested in the ever-expanding pool of blood, which had drained from the bullet hole in his right temple. A scarlet rivulet trailed down over the black eye-patch and onto the green desk-blotter. Glass's pale face was turned at such an angle that his open left eye, the one not concealed by the patch, seemed to be staring directly at a large notebook lying beside the steel tray. Aaron-

Smith's name was written on the cover; here were Martín's missing notes.

Holmes motioned me in; and with the aid of my stick, I carefully advanced toward the body. I felt for a pulse, but there was no doubt that he was dead. I shook my head and then with the same care retraced my steps back out the doorway.

Lewis, de Kruif and I watched Sherlock Holmes review the tableau in his usual manner, first examining the area surrounding the corpse, then inching his way towards the body itself. Holmes took out his lens and scrutinized the wound, studied the length of the dead man's extended arm, and sniffed at the gun barrel when he reached the floor. In reality, there seemed little need for any extensive detective work.

Before Holmes rang the police, he sent Lewis and De Kruif on their way.

On the pavement outside the surgery, we awaited the arrival of the authorities. After a few minutes had passed, a black police motor, an American-made Model-T Ford, pulled to the kerb in front of us. A large man with a sweeping moustache stepped out.

"Mr. Sherlock Holmes," exclaimed Chief Inspector Matthew Broadbent, touching the brim of his bowler.

Though Holmes had retired twenty years before, he had participated in enough investigations since then to be recognized by most members of the current police force. It was during one such investigation—the curious murder of a seller of antiquated sea charts—that I myself had met the Chief Inspector.

"So good to see you again, Holmes," Broadbent announced, a wide grin brightening his portly face. "Retirement treating you well, is it?"

Before Holmes could answer, however, the Chief Inspector changed his tone.

"Like old times, eh, Holmes?" he said coldly, the smile having left his lips. "A copper runs into you and says hello to some terrible crime, don't he? I understand there's a dead man inside."

"Indeed, Inspector," Holmes replied. "Dr. Timothy Glass. Watson and I"—at the mention of my name, Broadbent nodded his head towards me in a belated act of acknowledgement— "had come to ask Dr. Glass some questions. Just as we arrived, we heard a gunshot; and when there was no response to our rapping on his door, we broke it open. It was upon entering his surgery that we discovered the body."

"What sort of questions for the dead man did you have in mind then?" the policeman queried. "If you don't mind me asking."

Holmes nodded agreement. "Watson worked with Dr. Glass at Bart's in the fall of 1918, and we hoped for some information regarding the influenza."

Upon hearing the reference to the disastrous flu, the Chief Inspector shook his head. "Bad times, Holmes, that's for certain. Corpses right and left. Crime on the rise. That Spanish Lady was one she-devil I could have done without, I tell you that."

"The information we sought," Holmes explained, "was for an American acquaintance who is writing a book on the subject." Not only did Holmes fail to invoke Sinclair Lewis by name, but he also made no mention of the link to both Glass and the flu on the part of Sir Bernard Spilsbury. The pathologist's reputation would remain intact.

"A book about the flu?" Broadbent queried. "You must be joking." He laid his forefinger by the side of his nose. "Leave it to the Americans," he scoffed."

Broadbent waited a moment for us to embrace what he seemed to consider the wisdom of his last remark, then finally got down to business. "I should judge it is time to view the body." Nodding towards the building behind us, he asked, "What do you believe happened in there, Holmes? Your speculation might save me some trouble."

"I think you'll find it's all quite straight-forward, Chief Inspector. Before we ever arrived, the poor fellow took his own life with a bullet to the temple. Upon breaking in, Watson and I attempted to offer help—but to no avail. Clearly, a suicide. As for motive, a successful doctor like that? —I would not attempt to hazard a guess."

Broadbent eyed us suspiciously. "A total coincidence then, gentlemen—the fellow inside topping himself moments before you came to see him?" He paused to allow us a response. When there was none, he said, "The coroner will have a look, and there will be an inquest. No doubt, that will suffice. If need be, I'm sure I can count on you to appear."

As Holmes would soon be leaving London, I volunteered my own services; and Broadbent dismissed us with a wave of his hand. As we walked off, he turned round and, accompanied by a uniformed constable, took a deep breath, and entered the building.

Once it was clear that we had successfully dealt with the police, I was prepared to retrace our steps to Queen Anne Street. Holmes, however, surprised me with other plans.

"This has been a vexing afternoon, old fellow. I believe a change of scenery would be in order. Whilst you were searching the medical registry this morning, I was perusing *The Times* to learn what musical treasures might be in the offing. Its being a Monday, performances in London are scarce; but as it so happens, Sir Edward Elgar himself is conducting the music he composed for Binyon's play, *King Arthur.* The production appears tonight at the Old Vic. I fancy the steak and kidney pie at Rules would be just the thing to set matters right before we cross the river."

I could not disagree. What better place to begin expunging the afternoon's image of death than a plush, red-velvet booth among the dark-wood beams and the framed portraits that make up the *décor* of Rules? In particular, I trained my focus on the sticky toffee pudding with which I planned to conclude my meal.

The remainder of the day's agenda now set, Holmes hailed a cab, and we put the recent unpleasantness out of mind.

Chapter Ten

Resolution

The history of [a scientific experiment] is instructive, as it
warns us against considering problems as beyond our reach
because they have not yet found their solution.
--Jacques Loeb
*The Dynamics
of Living Matter*

"I suppose we owe Mr. Lewis a bit of
thanks," said Sherlock Holmes between bites of crisp
bacon the following morning.

Miss Ross had set before us a proper
English breakfast; and after she had finished serving,
Holmes and I began discussing the case.

"There would have been no investigation
into Aaron-Smith's murder," Holmes went on,
"without Lewis's stirring the pot with his questions."

"I shall certainly thank him if he comes
calling again."

Holmes smiled. "The unfortunate
suicide of Dr. Glass notwithstanding, you must feel
relieved to have learned once and for all that you were
not to blame for Aaron-Smith's death."

I cannot deny that I heard Holmes's words; and yet, though I might now exclude myself from blame, I could still not avoid revisiting the senseless demise of so promising a young man. After all, different circumstances might have allowed him to discover a cure for the Spanish flu or a remedy for some other terrible illness or even, simply, to have had a happy life with Miss Ross.

Holmes seemed to sense the depth of my feeling. At least, I interpreted his words in such a fashion when upon leaving for Victoria he added, "I do appreciate, old fellow, what a weight you have been carrying about."

Though neither Holmes nor I ever saw Sinclair Lewis or Paul de Kruif again, I did hear stories among the literati of a falling out between them. Apparently, Lewis had attempted to deny de Kruif the title of collaborator on the new novel the two of them had just completed together, a designation upon which both of them had previously agreed.

Ironically for one who had attacked the putative commercialism of the Rockefeller Institute, de Kruif did concede that equal billing might cause readers to think that Sinclair Lewis could no longer write on his own and thus hurt sales of the book. In the end, at the cost of their friendship, de Kruif accepted printed acknowledgement from Lewis for the so-called "help" de Kruif had contributed.

Despite the continuing discontent between the two Americans that the novel had engendered, I was pleased with my own response to Lewis's initial prodding. His persistence enabled me to separate myself from the many writers who have failed to confront their experiences during the pandemic of 1918 and in the process freed me from a mistaken belief that had haunted me for years. At the same time, without Lewis's questions, the reading public would never have learned the true story behind the genesis of his Pulitzer Prize-worthy work.

What is more, Sinclair Lewis thanked me for my effort. On a cold winter's morning in January of 1924, less than a year after the suicide of Timothy Glass, Miss Ross brought me a letter that had arrived earlier that day. The contents appeared in Lewis's informal epistolary style, and the envelope bore a postmark from nearby Chelsea. It was in Chelsea, I would later learn, that Lewis and Gracie, who had joined her husband the previous May, were spending the winter months. The letter had been posted just after the couple had returned to London following a tour of Italy.

John [the letter read], *I'm writing to thank you for your contribution to my latest novel—I completed the MS this past*

September. Convey the same appreciation to your detective-friend.

I also wanted to tell you about the new title I am considering for the book. From the start I told DeKruif that name-titles are best, & so I am planning to name the book after the protagonist. Usually, I pick random names from a telephone directory, but on this occasion, Gott sei Dank, I have too perfect a model from true life to ignore! Yuh, in memory of your deceased colleague, MarTIN Aaron-Smith, I have decided to call the book "Arrowsmith" . . . . (You might be interested to know that I have also appropriated the macabre story of the tainted cigarette to account for a major death in the plot.)

One of our magazines in NY plans to begin serializing Martin in June. As much as I hate carving up my work, they're telling me I'll have to make a number of cuts to conform to the magazine's requirements. To distinguish the book from the magazine version, I am titling the serial form "Dr. Martin Arrowsmith" & I hope to complete the editing by the end of April.

Here's a final tidbit that might interest you. Last month I wrote my publisher, Alf Harcourt, that after completing <u>Arrowsmith,</u> I have a couple of other projects in mind. I told him of "a lovely detective story" I was planning. . . . . . . But kindly inform your friend S. that it's NOT going to be about him.

[The letter was signed] *Red.*

THE END

Editor's Notes

The periodical, *The Designer and the Woman's Magazine,* was first to publish *Arrowsmith.* As Sinclair Lewis had written to Watson, although cut slightly and officially titled *Dr. Martin Arrowsmith* (to avoid confusion with the British publishing house called Arrowsmith), the novel appeared serially from June 1924 to April 1925. The complete novel was published in March 1925. As Watson reported, *Arrowsmith* won the Pulitzer Prize for Novels in 1926, but Lewis refused the award (and the $1000 that went with it).

Despite his letter to Alfred Harcourt in which Lewis revealed his plan for the book to follow *Arrowsmith,* his next novel turned out to be not a detective story at all, but a relatively unsuccessful romance titled *Mantrap* (1926).

For a greater understanding of the issues related to Watson's narrative, one must, of course, begin by reading *Arrowsmith.* For the story of Sinclair Lewis himself, see Mark Schorer's detailed biography, *Sinclair Lewis: A Life.* For insights into the relationship between Lewis and Paul de Kruif, see de Kruif's memoir, *The Sweeping Wind,* and the essay, "Sinclair Lewis, Paul de Kruif, and the

Composition of *Arrowsmith* by James M, Hutchisson (John Hopkins University Press, Spring 1992).

The following histories provide comprehensive information on the flu of 1918: *Living with Enza: The Forgotten Story of Britain and the Great Flu Pandemic of 1918* by Mark Honigsbaum and *Flu: The Story of the Great Influenza Pandemic of 1918, and the Search for the Virus that Caused It* by Gina Kolata.

To read Sir Arthur Conan Doyle's account of his communication with the spirit of his son, see "A Wonderful Séance" at arthur-conan-doyle.com.

For more on the life of pathologist Sir Bernard Spilsbury, see *Lethal Witness* by Andrew Ross and *The Father of Forensics* by Colin Evans. (Consistent with Watson's account, neither work mentions Holmes's aid in any of Spilsbury's cases.)

Finally, for specific discussions on the relationship between Sinclair Lewis and Sherlock Holmes, see the articles, "Sinclair Lewis, Max Gottlieb, and Sherlock Holmes" by Robert L. Coard in *Modern Fiction Studies*, Autumn 1985, and "Sherlock Holmes Meets Sinclair Lewis" by Martin Bucco in *The Sinclair Lewis Society Newsletter*, Fall 2000.

Also from Daniel D Victor

Sherlock Homes and The Shadows of St.Petersburg

"A psychological account of a crime" - that's how Fyodor
Dostoyevsky described his novel *Crime and Punishment*, which
tells of two horrific axe murders in St. Petersburg. It becomes much
more than a mere "account", however, when a pair of dead bodies
turn up in London's East End, their heads split open by an axe blade.

To Scotland Yard, the crimes are murders to solve. To Sherlock
Holmes, they present an intriguing puzzle. But to the literary man,
Dr. John H. Watson, they seem a deliberate restaging of the brutal
murders depicted in Dostoyevsky's narrative. If Watson is right,
what can be the purpose behind an actual recreation of the fictional
killings?

Blocking the answer to that question is a mysterious assortment of
English and Russian eccentrics, and one can only wonder if the
startling revelation at the end will be dramatic enough to set matters
straight.

MX Publishing

MX Publishing brings the best in new Sherlock Holmes novels, biographies, graphic novels and short story collections every month. With over 400 books it's the largest catalogue of new Sherlock Holmes books in the world.

We have over one hundred and fifty Holmes authors. The majority of our authors write new Holmes fiction - in all genres from very traditional pastiches through to modern novels, fantasy, crossover, children's books and humour.

In Holmes biography we have award winning historians including Alistair Duncan, Paul R Spiring, and Brian W Pugh

MX Publishing also has one of the largest communities of Holmes fans on Facebook and Twitter under @mxpublishing.

www.mxpublishing.com

Also from MX Publishing

When the papal apartments are burgled in 1901, Sherlock Holmes is summoned to Rome by Pope Leo XII. After learning from the pontiff that several priceless cameos that could prove compromising to the church, and perhaps determine the future of the newly unified Italy, have been stolen, Holmes is asked to recover them. In a parallel story, Michelangelo, the toast of Rome in 1501 after the unveiling of his Pieta, is commissioned by Pope Alexander VI, the last of the Borgia pontiffs, with creating the cameos that will bedevil Holmes and the papacy four centuries later. For fans of Conan Doyle's immortal detective, the game is always afoot. However, the great detective has never encountered an adversary quite like the one with whom he crosses swords in "The Vatican Cameos.."

"An extravagantly imagined and beautifully written Holmes story"

(Lee Child, NY Times Bestselling author,
Jack Reacher series)

Also from MX Publishing

Our bestselling books are our short story collections;

'Lost Stories of Sherlock Holmes' , 'The Outstanding Mysteries of Sherlock Holmes', The Papers of Sherlock Holmes Volume 1 and 2, 'Untold Adventures of Sherlock Holmes' (and the sequel 'Studies in Legacy) and 'Sherlock Holmes in Pursuit', 'The Cotswold Werewolf and Other Stories of Sherlock Holmes' – and many more......

Also from MX Publishing

"Phil Growick's, 'The Secret Journal of Dr Watson', is an adventure which takes place in the latter part of Holmes and Watson's lives. They are entrusted by HM Government (although not officially) and the King no less to undertake a rescue mission to save the Romanovs, Russia's Royal family from a grisly end at the hand of the Bolsheviks. There is a wealth of detail in the story but not so much as would detract us from the enjoyment of the story. Espionage, counter-espionage, the ace of spies himself, double-agents, double-crossers...all these flit across the pages in a realistic and exciting way. All the characters are extremely well-drawn and Mr Growick, most importantly, does not falter with a very good ear for Holmesian dialogue indeed. Highly recommended. A five-star effort."
The Baker Street Society

www.ingramcontent.com/pod-product-compliance
Lightning Source LLC
Chambersburg PA
CBHW030347180626
46812CB00007B/2786